Welcome to the world of
St Piran's Hospital—

Next to the rugged shores of Penhally Bay
lies the picturesque Cornish town of St Piran,
where you'll find a bustling hospital famed
for the dedication, talent and passion
of its staff—on and off the wards!

Under the warmth of the Cornish sun,
Italian doctors, heart surgeons and
playboy princes discover that romance blossoms
in the most unlikely of places…

You'll also meet the devilishly handsome
Dr Josh O'Hara and the beautiful,
fragile Megan Phillips…and discover the secret
that tore these star-crossed lovers apart.

Turn the page to step into St Piran's—
where every drama has a dreamy doctor…
and a happy ending.

Dear Reader

I was so pleased to be asked to be part of the *St Piran's Hospital* series, as I really enjoyed taking part in the last two series set in Penhally Bay. Between us, we authors developed such a lovely warm community—the kind of place where we all said we'd really like to live—that it was great to come back to both Penhally and its major hospital, further along the Cornish coast. I always enjoy revisiting old characters, so you might recognise a couple here, and I had a lot of fun getting the pin-up local firefighter together with the very shy, very sweet school nurse. Not to mention having a great excuse to chat to my Medical™ Romance author friends—all in the name of research and discussing the series, of course…

It's a story of finding love in unexpected places, and learning how to make a family. And I thoroughly enjoyed joining Tom on his rescues, and getting him to show Flora who she really is. Not to mention reliving bits of my children's early childhood; some of our favourite trips inspired the family outings that Flora, Tom and Joey have! You'll need a few tissues, in places, but I hope you'll find bits that make you smile, too.

I'm always delighted to hear from readers, so do come and visit me at www.katehardy.com

With love

Kate Hardy

ST PIRAN'S: THE FIREMAN AND NURSE LOVEDAY

BY
KATE HARDY

All the characters in this book have no existence outside the imagination of the author, and have no relation whatsoever to anyone bearing the same name or names. They are not even distantly inspired by any individual known or unknown to the author, and all the incidents are pure invention.

First published in Great Britain 2011
Harlequin Mills & Boon Limited,
Eton House, 18-24 Paradise Road, Richmond, Surrey TW9 1SR

© Harlequin Books S.A. 2011

ISBN: 978 0 263 88586 6

Special thanks and acknowledgement are given to Pamela Brooks for her contribution to the *St Piran's Hospital* series

Harlequin Mills & Boon policy is to use papers that are natural, renewable and recyclable products and made from wood grown in sustainable forests. The logging and manufacturing process conform to the legal environmental regulations of the country of origin.

Printed and bound in Spain
by Litografia Rosés, S.A., Barcelona

ST PIRAN'S HOSPITAL
*Where every drama has a dreamy doctor...
and a happy ending.*

*In December we gave you the first two St Piran's stories
in one month!*

**Nick Tremayne and Kate Althorp
finally got their happy-ever-after in:**
ST PIRAN'S: THE WEDDING OF THE YEAR
by Caroline Anderson

**Dr Izzy Bailey was swept off her feet
by sexy Spaniard Diego Ramirez**
ST PIRAN'S: RESCUING PREGNANT CINDERELLA
by Carol Marinelli

**In January the arrival of sizzlingly hot
Italian neurosurgeon Giovanni Corezzi
was enough to make any woman forget the cold!**
ST PIRAN'S: ITALIAN SURGEON, FORBIDDEN BRIDE
by Margaret McDonagh

**In February daredevil doc William MacNeil
unexpectedly discovered he was a father in:**
ST PIRAN'S: DAREDEVIL, DOCTOR...DAD!
by Anne Fraser

**March saw a new heart surgeon
who had everyone's pulses racing in:**
ST PIRAN'S: THE BROODING HEART SURGEON
by Alison Roberts

**This month fireman Tom Nicholson
steals Flora Loveday's heart in:**
ST PIRAN'S: THE FIREMAN AND NURSE LOVEDAY
by Kate Hardy

**Newborn twins could just bring a May marriage miracle
for Brianna and Connor**
ST PIRAN'S: TINY MIRACLE TWINS
by Maggie Kingsley

**And playboy Prince Alessandro Cavalieri
honours St Piran's with a visit in June**
ST PIRAN'S: PRINCE ON THE CHILDREN'S WARD
by Sarah Morgan

CHAPTER ONE

THE familiar warble flooded through the fire station and the Tannoy gave a high-pitched whine.

Was it a drill, Tom wondered, at 2:00 p.m. on a Friday afternoon?

And then he heard the words, 'Turnout, vehicles 54 and 55. Fire at Penhally Bay Primary School. Query trapped children.'

Joey's school.

Fear lanced through him. Please, God, let this be a drill.

Except he knew it wasn't. Their drill was always a fire at 3 King Street, St Piran—which just so happened to be the address of the main fire station in the area. Which meant that this was real.

He headed straight for engine 54, where the rest of the crew were already stepping into their protective trousers, jackets and boots. Steve, the station manager, was in the front seat, tapping into the computer and checking the details.

'What have we got, Guv?' Tom asked as he swung into the seat next to Steve, the doors went up and the engine sped down the road towards Penhally Bay.

Steve checked the computer screen. 'Explosion and fire at Penhally Bay Primary.' He gave the driver, Gary, the map reference, even though everyone knew exactly where the school was, on the hill overlooking the bay. 'Called in by Rosemary

Bailey, the headmistress. The fire's in a corridor by a storeroom and it's blocked off three rooms. Two of the classes were out, so that leaves the quiet room and the toilets. They're still checking off the kids' names, so they're not sure right now if anyone's in there or not.' He paused. 'The storeroom contains all the art stuff, so we're talking about flammable hazards and possible chemical inhalation from glue and what have you. Tom, you're lead. Roy, you're BAECO.' The breathing apparatus entry co-ordinator kept the control board with the firefighters' tallies in place so he knew who was in the building, how long they'd been in there, and when he needed to call them out because their oxygen supplies would be starting to run low.

'The rest of you, follow Tom's lead. We'll start with the tanks in the appliances, then we'll set the hydrant and check the supply.'

'Right, Guv,' the crew chorused.

'Who's our back-up?' Tom asked. Two engines were always sent out for an initial call, and then more would be called as needed, staggering their arrival.

'King Street's on standby,' Steve said. 'And the paramedics are on their way.'

All standard stuff, Tom knew.

'Nick Tremayne is going to be there, too,' Steve added.

Tom had attended fires with Nick in attendance before, and knew that the GP was unflappable and worked well in a crisis. 'That's good.' And Tom was really relieved that his crew was taking the call, so he could see for himself that his nephew was fine.

And Joey *would* be fine.

He had to be.

Joey was all Tom had left of his big sister since the car accident that had claimed her life and her husband's just over a month ago, at New Year. Losing her had ripped Tom's heart to shreds; the idea of anything happening to his precious nephew, the little boy his sister had entrusted to his care…

His mind closed, refusing to even consider the idea. Joey couldn't be one of the trapped children. He just *couldn't*.

But, all the way there, Tom was horribly aware of the extra problems that small children brought to a fire. Physically, their bodies couldn't cope as well as an adult's with the heat of a raging fire. And then there was the fear factor. Everyone was scared in a fire—you couldn't see your hand in front of your face, thanks to the choking thick smoke, and the heat and noise were incredible. Children found it even harder to cope with the way their senses were overwhelmed, and sometimes got to the point where they simply couldn't follow directions because they were too frightened to listen.

Please, God, let Joey be safe, he prayed silently. *Please*.

'Hello, Tommy,' Flora said as Trish Atkins, the teacher of the three-year-olds, brought the next of her charges through to the quiet room where Flora was giving the routine vaccinations. She smiled at the little boy. 'I know Mummy told you why I've come to see your class today—not with my magic measuring tape to see how tall you all are, but to give you two injections to stop you catching a bug and getting sick.'

Tommy nodded. 'Will they hurt?'

'You'll feel a bit of a scratch,' she said, 'and it's OK to say a big "Ow" and hold Trish's hand really tightly, but it'll be over really quickly and I'll need you to stay still for me. Can you do that?'

'Yes,' he lisped.

'Good boy.' She gave him the choice of which arm and where he wanted to sit; he opted to sit on Trish's lap.

'Mummy told me you're getting a kitten.' Distraction was a brilliant technique; if she could get him chatting about the new addition to their family, he wouldn't focus on the vaccination syringe and he'd feel it as the scratch she'd promised, rather than as a terrifying pain. 'What's he like?'

'He's black.'

'What are you going to call him?'

'Ow!' Tommy's lower lip wobbled when the needle went in, but then he said, 'Smudge. 'Cause he's got a big white smudge on his back.'

'That's a great name.' She smiled at him. 'What sort of toys are you going to get him?'

'A squeaky red mouse,' Tommy said. 'Ow!'

'All done—and you were so brave that I'm going to give you a sticker. Do you want to choose one?'

The distraction of a shiny rocket sticker made Tommy forget about crying, just as Flora had hoped it would. She updated his notes, and was about to put her head round the door of the quiet room to tell Trish that she was ready for the next child when she heard a huge bang and then fire alarms going off.

She left her papers where they were and headed out to the main rooms of the nursery. The children were all filing out into the garden, some of the younger ones crying and holding the hands of the class assistants. Flora could see through the large windows that Christine Galloway, the head of the nursery, was taking a roll-call of all the staff and children.

'I think everyone's out, but I'm checking nobody's been left behind,' Trish said from the far end of the room.

'Do you want me to check the toilets?' Flora asked.

'Yes, please.' Trish gave her a grateful smile.

Once they were both satisfied that everyone was out, Flora grabbed her medical kit and they joined Christine and the other teachers. Two fire engines roared up, sirens blaring and blue lights flashing, and they could see smoke coming over the fence from the primary school next door.

'I'd better get next door in case anyone's hurt and they need medical help,' Flora said, biting her lip. She knew all the children in the school, from her work as the school liaison nurse, and the idea of any of them being hurt or, even worse… *No*. It was unthinkable.

'Let us know if there's anything we can do,' Christine said. 'I'll put your notes in my office when we can go back into the building.'

'Thanks.' Flora gave her a quick smile, then hurried next door to the primary school.

The first person she saw was her boss, Nick Tremayne, the head of the surgery in the village. 'Nick, what's happened? I was next door doing the vaccinations when I heard a bang and the fire alarms went off.'

'We don't know what caused it—only that there's a fire.' Nick gestured to the firemen pumping water onto the building.

'Is anyone hurt?'

'Right now, we're not sure. The head's getting everyone out and ticking off names.'

Flora glanced at the building and saw where the flames were coming out. 'That's the corridor by the art storeroom— it's full of stuff that could go up.' And she really, really hoped that everyone was out of the block. The corridor led to the storeroom and three prefab rooms. Two of the rooms were used as Year Five classrooms and the third was used as the quiet room, where teachers took children for extra reading practice or tests.

The firefighters were already working to quell the blaze. Some had breathing apparatus on, and others were putting water on the blaze. She could hear one of the fire crew yelling instructions about a hydrant.

Before she could ask Nick anything else, two ambulances screamed up. The paramedic crew and two doctors headed towards them. Flora recognised one of them as Megan Phillips, who lived in the village, though she didn't know Megan's colleague.

'I'm Josh O'Hara, A and E consultant,' the unknown doctor introduced himself. 'And this is Megan Phillips, paediatrician.'

Josh was simply gorgeous, with black tousled hair that flopped in his indigo-blue eyes. Right now he wasn't smiling; but no doubt when he did, any woman under the age of ninety would feel her heart turning over. And that Irish brogue would definitely melt hearts.

Although Flora knew who Megan was, she didn't know the doctor well at all; Megan kept herself very much to herself in the village. So Flora was relieved when Nick stepped in and spoke for both of them. 'Nick Tremayne, head of Penhally Bay Surgery—and this is Flora, my practice nurse and school liaison. Luckily she was doing the MMR vaccinations next door and she's brilliant with kids. Flora, you know Megan, don't you? Can you work with her and I'll work with Josh?'

'Yes, of course,' Flora said.

Though she also noticed that Megan and Josh didn't glance at each other, the way that colleagues usually did. The tension between them was obvious, so either they hadn't worked together before and weren't sure of each other's skills, or they knew each other and really didn't get on. Well, whatever it was, she hoped they'd manage to put it aside and work together until everyone was safe. In this situation, the children really had to come first.

Megan gave her a slightly nervous smile. 'Shall we go and see what's going on?'

Flora nodded. 'The fire drill point's at the far end of the playground, on the other side of the building.'

'We'll start there, then, and see if anyone needs treating,' Megan said. 'As you're school liaison, you must know everyone here?'

Flora felt colour flooding into her cheeks, and sighed inwardly. If only she didn't blush so easily. She knew it made her look like a bumbling fool, and she wasn't. She was a good nurse and she was fine with the children—and the teachers, now she'd got to know them. She just found herself shy and tongue-tied with adults she didn't know very well. Stupid, at her age, she knew, but she couldn't help it. Pulling herself together, she said, 'I know all the staff and most of the children—I've either worked with their class or seen them for the usual check-ups.'

'That's good—you'll be a familiar face and that will help them feel less scared,' Megan said.

As they rounded the corner, they could see a woman leaning against the wall, her face white, nursing her arm.

'Patience, this is Megan, one of the doctors from St Piran's. Megan, this is Patience Harcourt. She teaches Year Three,' Flora introduced them swiftly. 'Patience, what's happened to your arm?'

'I'd gone to the storeroom to get some supplies. I'd just switched on the light when it went bang—I went straight for the fire extinguisher, but before I could do anything the whole thing went up. I got out of there and closed the fire door to contain it.' She grimaced. 'Thank goodness one of the Year Five classes was doing PE and the other was in the ICT suite.'

'Was anyone in the quiet room?' Flora asked.

Patience shook her head, looking white. 'I hope not, but I don't know.'

'Let's have a look at your arm,' Megan said, and sucked in a breath. 'That's a nasty burn.'

Patience made a dismissive gesture with her other arm. 'I can wait. Check the children over first.'

'Your burn needs dressing—the sooner, the better,' Megan said gently. 'Will you let Flora do it while I check the children?'

The children were shivering because it was cold outside and the teachers had taken them straight outside away from the fire, not stopping to pick up coats; some were still wearing their PE kit. Some were crying, and all were clearly frightened.

'We need to get them huddled together to conserve warmth,' Megan said. 'Under that shelter would be good. And then I can see if anyone needs treating. Flora, when you've dressed Patience's burn, do you want to come and help me?'

'Will do.' Again, Flora could feel the hated colour flood her cheeks. She was glad of the excuse to turn her face away while she delved in her medical kit; then brought out what she needed to dress the burn and make Patience more comfortable.

Tom was training one of the hoses on the flames. He didn't have a clue whether Joey was safely in the playground with the other children because he couldn't see. Although he was frantic to know that Joey was all right, he had a job to do and his colleagues were relying on him not to let them down. He had to keep doing his job and trust his colleagues to do theirs.

I swear if he's safe then I'll do better by him, he promised silently to his sister. I'll change my job, give up firefighting and concentrate on him.

And then the headmistress hurried over towards them.

'Is everyone safe?' Steve asked.

Rosemary Bailey looked grim. 'There's still part of one class missing. Some of the Reception children.'

Tom, overhearing her, went cold. *Joey was in the Reception year.* 'Is Joey all right?' he asked urgently.

Rosemary bit her lip. 'He's not with the others. There's a group of children who'd gone to the quiet room at the end for extra help with reading. He must be with them.'

Tom swallowed hard. 'The quiet room. Is that the room at the end of the corridor?' The room that was cut off, right now, by flames.

'Yes.'

'It's near the storeroom where the fire started. Right now, it's structurally unstable,' Steve said. 'How many children are there?'

'Five, plus Matty Roper, the teaching assistant in R2.'

R2. Definitely Joey's class, Tom knew. And he knew Matty—he'd had twice-weekly meetings with her about Joey since he'd become Joey's guardian. Joey had been struggling at school for the last month, just shutting off, so Tom and Matty had been trying to work out how they could help him settle back in.

Ice slid through his veins. The children were stranded. *Including Joey.*

CHAPTER TWO

'RIGHT, I'm going in,' Tom said. 'Gary, can you take this hose from me?'

Steve grabbed Tom's shoulder to stop him. 'You're not going anywhere.'

'My nephew's trapped in that room. No way in hell am I leaving him there!' Tom snarled back.

'Nobody's saying that you have to leave him, Tom. But nobody's going into that corridor until we've stabilised the area—otherwise the whole lot could come down. And we can't afford to let the flames reach the really flammable stuff.'

Steve was making absolute sense. As an experienced fireman and the station manager, he knew exactly what he was doing. Tom was well aware of that. And yet every nerve in his body rebelled against his boss's orders. How could he just wait outside when his nephew was trapped inside that room?

'Tom, I know you think Joey might be in there, but you can't afford to let emotion get in the way.'

Ordinarily, Tom didn't. He was able to distance himself from things and stay focused, carrying others through a crisis situation with his calm strength. But this was different. This was Joey. The last link to his elder sister. No way could he let the little boy down.

'You either keep doing your job as lead fireman and getting

the flames under control,' Steve said softly, 'or you're off duty as of now, which means you go back to the station.'

And then it would be even longer before he could find out if Joey was safe. Waiting would drive him crazy. Tom dragged in a breath. 'Right, Guv. I'm sticking to my post.'

The fire crew that had arrived as back-up started to get the supports up; Tom forced himself to concentrate on damping down the blaze. Abandoning his job wouldn't help Joey. Focus, he told himself. Just *focus*.

It felt like a lifetime, but at last the area was stabilised and they were in a position to rescue the trapped children and their teacher. Steve had already vetoed the door as the access point; although the flames were out, the corridor was still thick with smoke, and until the fire had been damped down properly it could reignite at any time. The window was the safest option, now the area was stabilised.

But there was no way Tom's muscular frame would fit through the window. His colleagues, too, were brawny and would find it an equally tight fit.

'Um, excuse me?'

Tom looked down at the woman standing next to him. She was a foot shorter than him, and her face was bright red—whether through embarrassment or the heat from the fire, he had no idea.

'I'm the school nurse,' she said. 'Look, I know I'm a bit, um, round...' her colour deepened and she looked at the floor '...and I'm not as strong as you, but the children are only little. Matty and I can lift them up between us and pass them through to you. And I can check them over while I'm in there and make sure they're all right.'

'I see where you're coming from,' he said, 'but you're a civilian. I can't let you take that risk.'

'But I know the children,' she said, her voice earnest—though she still wasn't looking at him, Tom noticed. 'It'll be less frightening for them if I go in to help.' She bit her lip. 'I know it's dangerous, but I won't do anything reckless. And we need to get the children out quickly.'

True. And, the faster they did that, the sooner he'd see Joey. That was the clincher for him. 'All right. Thank you.'

She nodded. 'I'm sorry I'm, um, a bit heavy.'

He looked at her properly then. Yes, she was curvy. Plump, if he was brutally honest. But there was a sweetness and kindness in her face, a genuine desire to help—something that he knew had been missing from the other women he'd dated. Sure, they might have been tall and leggy and jaw-droppingly gorgeous, but they would've fussed about chipping a nail. And he knew who he'd rather have beside him in this crisis. Definitely the school nurse.

And she had the sweetest, softest mouth. A mouth that made him want to…

Whatever was the *matter* with him? His nephew was missing, he had a job to do, and he was thinking about what it would be like to kiss a complete stranger? For pity's sake—he needed to concentrate!

'You're fine,' he said, and proved it by lifting her up to the window as if she weighed no more than a feather.

She scrambled through, and Tom almost forgot to breathe while he waited. Were the children all right? Was Joey safe?

And then Matty Roper and the school nurse came to the window and started lifting the children through, and there just wasn't time to ask about Joey as he took the children one by one and passed them over to the team of medics lining up behind him ready to check over the children.

Three.

Four.

He swallowed hard. The next one would be Joey.

Except the next person to come to the window was Matty Roper.

'Where's Joey?' he asked urgently. 'The head said there were five children missing—that they were in the quiet room with you.'

'Only four,' Matty said. 'And Joey wasn't one of them.'

'But he *has* to be. There were five children missing. He was one of them.'

'I'm sorry, Tom. I only took four children to the quiet room with me and they're all accounted for.'

Panic flowed through him, making every muscle feel like lead. How could Joey be missing? How?

'Please, Matty. Check again. Just in case he came in and you didn't see him.'

'Tom, I know he didn't,' Matty said gently. 'I'm sorry.'

'Then where the hell is he?' Tom burst out in desperation.

'I don't know.' She looked nervously at the supports against the wall. 'Is this going to hold?'

This was his job. He had to get Matty and the school nurse out. And then he could start to look for Joey.

Please, God, let it not be too late.

Grim-faced, he helped Matty through the window, and then the nurse.

Once they were both standing on safe ground, he leaned through the window. 'Joey! Joey, where are you?'

No answer.

Was he trapped in one of the other classrooms? 'Joey!' he bellowed.

'Do you mean Joey Barber?' the nurse asked.

'Yes.' She'd seen the other children, Tom thought, so maybe she'd seen his nephew. 'Have you seen him?'

She shook her head. 'Not today.' Again, she didn't meet his

eyes. 'He's the little boy who lost his parents just after New Year, isn't he?'

'My sister and her husband,' Tom confirmed. And it was beginning to look as if Joey might be joining his parents. No, no, no. It couldn't happen. He couldn't bear it. 'The head said there were five children missing. Now it's just Joey. Oh, hell, can't he hear me? Why isn't he answering?' He yelled Joey's name again.

The nurse squeezed his hand. 'The noise of the explosion will have scared him and probably brought back memories of the car crash. Right now, even if he can hear you, he's probably too scared to answer.'

He thought about it and realised that she was right. 'Not that he speaks much anyway, since the accident,' Tom said wryly. 'He barely strings two words together now. It's been so hard to reach him since Susie and Kevin died.' He dragged in a breath. 'If anything's happened to him, I'll never forgive myself.' He'd never be able to live with the guilt: his sister had asked him to look after her precious child, and he'd failed. Big time.

'This isn't your fault,' she said softly. 'You can't blame yourself.'

'I need to find him.' He handed over his damping-down duties to one of his colleagues and went in search of the station manager. 'Guv, Joey's still missing. I need to find him. Please.'

'All right.' Steve looked at him, grim-faced. 'But you don't take *any* risks, you hear me?'

'I won't,' Tom promised. He wouldn't put anyone in danger. But he'd take the buildings apart with his bare hands if he had to, to find his nephew.

'I, um, could help you look for him, if you like.' The nurse was by his side again. 'He knows me, and a familiar face might help.'

'Thank you.' Tom looked at her. 'I don't even know your name,' he blurted out.

'Flora. Flora Loveday.' Her face reddened again. 'And I know it's a stupid name. I'm not a delicate little flower.'

'No.' He was beginning to realise now that she was shy, like the proverbial violet—that was why she blushed and couldn't quite get her words out and found it hard to look him in the eye—but he had a feeling that there was much more to Flora Loveday than that. She'd put herself in a dangerous situation to help the children. 'No, you're like a…a peony,' Tom said, thinking of the flowers his mother had always grown in summer. 'Brave and bright and strong.'

Her blush deepened to the point where she seriously resembled the flower.

'I'm Tom. Tom Nicholson.'

She nodded but said nothing and looked away.

With Flora by his side, he checked with Rosemary Bailey and the rest of the fire crew. All the areas had been cleared, and nobody had seen Joey.

He eyed the wreckage. Fear tightened round his chest, to the point where he could barely breathe. Where was Joey? 'Maybe he's in the toilets,' he said.

Flora shook her head. 'They've been checked.'

'He has to be here. He *has* to be.' Desperately, he yelled Joey's name again.

'If he's scared already, shouting is only going to make him panic more,' she said quietly. She paused. 'When I was Joey's age, I hated going to school. I used to hide in the cloakrooms.'

Tom hardly dared hope that Joey would've done the same. But it was the best option he had right now. 'Let's have another look. I know they've been checked, but…' He glanced over to the huddled children at the far end of the playground.

'Joey's tiny. If he was sitting among the coats and didn't reply, whoever checked might have missed him.'

Together, they went over to the Reception cloakrooms.

'I'll start this end—can you start that end, Flora?' Tom asked.

'Sure.'

He'd checked under every coat at his end when he heard Flora call out, 'He's here.'

Huddled up at the far end of the cloakroom, beneath piles of coats, his nephew was white-faced. And Tom had never been so glad to see him in all his life. He dropped to his knees and hugged the little boy tightly, uncaring that he was covered in smoke and smuts and he would make Joey's clothes filthy.

Joey squirmed. 'You're hurting me,' he whispered.

The soft sound pierced Tom's heart. Of course. The little boy didn't like being touched, not since his parents had died. As a toddler, he'd adored riding on his uncle's shoulders and playing football and going down the huge slide in the playground on Tom's or his father's lap, but since the accident he'd put huge barriers round himself.

Tom let his nephew go. 'Sorry, Jojo. I didn't mean to hurt you. It's just I was very scared when I couldn't find you. I'm so glad you're all right.'

Joey stared at him and said nothing.

'I know this afternoon's been scary, but it's all going to be just fine,' Tom said softly. 'I promise. I'm going to have to stay here until the fire's completely out and everything's safe, but maybe Mrs Bailey will let you sit in her office and do some drawing until I can get in touch with the childminder and see if she can take you home.'

Joey said nothing, and Tom had absolutely no idea what the little boy was thinking. Did he feel abandoned, or could he understand that other people relied on Tom to do his job and keep them safe and he had to share Tom's time?

Flora was sitting on the low bench by the coat rack. 'Or,' she said, 'maybe you could come home with me until your uncle's finished here. I live on a farm, and I've got the nicest dog in the world.'

Tom looked at her. 'But I've only just met you.' Did she really think he'd let his precious nephew go off with a complete stranger—even if she had been brilliant and helped to rescue him?

She bit her lip. 'I know, but Joey knows me. And my boss is here—I take it you know Nick Tremayne?' At Tom's curt nod, she said, 'He'll vouch for me. And it's no trouble. I just need to pick up my paperwork from the nursery next door—the children will all have gone home by now, so I'll have to finish the clinic next week anyway.'

So she *did* think he'd let Joey go home with someone he didn't know.

Then again, Tom was usually a good judge of character and he liked what he'd seen of Flora. She was kind, she was brave, and she'd thought of the children before herself.

'Is that all right with you, Joey?' Tom asked.

Joey looked wary, and Tom was about to refuse the offer when Flora said, 'You can meet my dog and see around the farm.'

'Dog,' Joey said.

And, for the first time in a long, long time, he gave a smile. A smile that vanished the second after it started, but it was a proper smile. And it made Tom's decision suddenly easy.

'Do you want to go with Flora and see her dog, Jojo?' Tom asked.

This time, Joey nodded.

'I can borrow a car seat from the nursery—they have spares,' Flora said. She took a notepad from her pocket and scribbled quickly on it. 'That's my address, my home phone and my mobile phone.'

'Thank you.' Tom dragged in a breath. 'This is going to sound really ungrateful. My instincts tell me to trust you, but—'

'I'm a stranger,' she finished. 'You can never take risks with children. They're too precious.' She bit her lip and looked away, and Tom felt like an utter heel. She was trying to help and he'd practically thrown the offer back in her face.

'Talk to Nick,' she said. 'And then, if you're happy for Joey to come with me, I'll be next door at the nursery.'

Somehow, she'd understood that this wasn't personal—that he'd be the same even if the offer had come from a teaching assistant he didn't know. 'Thank you,' Tom said and, making sure Joey was right by his side, went to find Nick Tremayne.

At half past seven that evening, Flora heard the car tyres on the gravel and glanced across at Banjo, who was standing guard over the child asleep on the beanbag. 'All right, boy. I heard him. Shh, now. Let Joey sleep.'

She'd opened the kitchen door before Tom could ring the doorbell. 'Joey's asleep in front of the fire,' she whispered. 'Come in.'

He'd showered and changed; out of his uniform, and with his face no longer covered by a mask and soot, Tom Nicholson was breathtakingly handsome. When he smiled at her, her heart actually skipped a beat.

Which was ridiculous, because he was way, *way* out of her league. He probably had a girlfriend already; though, even if he didn't, Flora knew he wouldn't look twice at her. Looking the way he did, and doing the job he did, Tom was probably used to scores of much more attractive women falling in a heap at his feet. He wouldn't be interested in a shy, plump nurse who spent most of her time looking like a beetroot.

'He's absolutely sound asleep,' Tom whispered, looking

down at his nephew, who was lying on the beanbag with a fleecy blanket tucked round him.

'It's been a long day for him—and a scary one.' She glanced at Tom. 'Um, I've already fed him. I hope that's OK.'

'That's great. Thanks for being so kind,' Tom said.

'I could hardly let him starve.' Flora shrugged it off. 'Poor little lad. He's had a lot to cope with, losing both his parents. I know what that's like.' She'd had to face losing both her parents, the previous year, so she had an idea what he was going through—though, being twenty years older than Joey, at least she'd had an adult's perspective to help her cope. She looked more closely at Tom and saw the lines of strain around his eyes. 'You look exhausted.'

'Once the immediate danger's passed, the real work starts—making sure we keep the site damped down so the fire doesn't flare up again.' Tom grimaced. 'Sorry I've been so long. And I took time out for a shower, because if I turned up covered in smuts and stinking of smoke it might scare Joey.'

He'd put his nephew first; and no doubt the shower had been at the expense of taking time to grab a meal. It was good that he could put Joey first, but the poor man must be starving as well as tired. And if she made him something to eat, she could keep herself busy doing something practical—which was a lot easier than sitting down and having a conversation where she'd end up blushing and stumbling over her words and getting flustered. She'd learned the hard way that being practical and doing something was the best way of dealing with her hated shyness. 'He's perfectly safe and comfortable where he is, so why don't you sit down and I'll make you a hot drink and something to eat?' Flora asked.

'I can't impose on you like that.'

'You're not imposing. I made a big batch of spaghetti sauce this afternoon. It won't take long to heat it through and cook some pasta—that's what Joey and I had.'

'Thank you.'

The next thing Tom knew, he was sitting at the table with a mug of coffee in front of him and Flora was pottering round the kitchen.

The kindness of a stranger. Tom was used to women offering to cook him things—it was a standing joke at the fire station that, almost every day, someone dropped by with a tin of home-made cookies or cakes or muffins for Tom. Old ladies whose cats he'd rescued, young mums whose toddlers he'd got out of a locked bathroom—and even the hard-nosed local reporter had seen him in action, rescuing someone from a burning building, and had joined what his crew-mates teasingly called the Tom Nicholson Fan Club, turning up with a batch of cookies for him on more than one occasion.

Even though he'd explained gently that he was simply doing his job, he could hardly be rude enough to turn away things that people had spent time making personally for him. So he accepted them with a smile on behalf of the fire crew, wrote thank-you notes—again on behalf of the entire fire crew—and secretly rather enjoyed them making a fuss over him.

But Flora Loveday was different.

There was something about her—a kind of inner peace and strength that drew him. Here, on her home ground, she glowed. He'd been too frantic with worry about Joey to notice properly earlier, but she was beautiful. Soft, gentle brown eyes; her hair, too, was soft, all ruffled and curly and cute. And the warmth she exuded made him want to hold her close, feel some of that warmth seeping into him and taking the chill of the fear away…

And then he realised what he was thinking and slammed the brakes on. Yes, he found her attractive—dangerously so—but he couldn't act on it. In his job, it wasn't fair to have a serious relationship with someone. He worked crazy hours and did dangerous things; he'd seen too many friends die and leave families behind. And there was Joey to consider, too. He'd had too many changes in his young life, just recently. The last thing he needed was his uncle being distracted by a new girlfriend.

But Tom also knew that he could do with a friend. Flora was the first person who'd seemed to understand or who had managed to start to reach Joey. And he really, really needed help reaching his nephew.

'So what have you and Joey been up to?' he asked.

'I took him to see the chickens.'

'Chickens?' He hadn't expected that.

She went pink again. 'My dad started Loveday Eggs.'

He'd seen their boxes in the shops. 'So you have chickens here?'

She nodded. 'The hens are free range, so we went and collected some eggs. And then we made some brownies.' She smiled. 'There are some left. But not that many.' She placed a bowl of pasta in front of him.

'This smells amazing. Thank you.' He took a mouthful. 'Wow. And it tastes even better than it smells.'

'It's only boring old spaghetti and sauce.' She looked away.

'It's wonderful.' He ate the lot and accepted a second bowl. And then he grimaced. 'Sorry. I've just been horribly greedy.'

'You've just spent hours sorting out a fire. You must've been starving.'

'I was,' he admitted. And then he accepted her offer of helping himself to the brownies. 'Wow. These are seriously good. And you made them with Joey?'

She fished her mobile phone out of her handbag, fiddled with it and then handed it to him. There was a picture of Joey, wearing a tea-towel as a makeshift apron, stirring the chocolatey mixture in a big bowl—and there was almost as much chocolate round his face.

And he looked happy.

Tom couldn't speak for a moment. Then he gulped in a breath. 'I didn't know Joey liked cooking.'

'Most kids love messy stuff,' she explained, her colour deepening. 'And cooking's better still because they get to eat what they make.'

In one afternoon, she seemed to have got far closer to his nephew than he'd managed in a month. And he knew he needed help. Flora might be the one to help him reach Joey—and there was just something about her that made Tom sure that she wouldn't judge him harshly. 'It never even occurred to me to try doing something like that with Joey.' He raked a hand through his hair. 'Don't get me wrong, I like kids. I'm always the one sent on school visits, but I just don't seem to be able to connect with Joey—and I'm his uncle. Everything I suggest us doing, he just stares at me and says nothing. I can't reach him any more. I feel…' He shook his head, grimacing. 'Hopeless. Helpless. I don't even know where to start.'

'Give it time,' she said. 'It's only been a month since the accident—and he was one of the quieter ones in the school even before then.'

Tom blinked in surprise. 'So you work at the school? I thought you said Nick Tremayne was your boss?'

'He is, but I'm the school liaison,' she explained.

'So you visit the local schools?'

She nodded. 'I spend half my time at the local nursery and schools, and half my time at the practice. I do a health visitor clinic at the primary school for mums one morning a week, a clinic at the high school, and I do the vaccinations and preschool health checks in the nursery. Plus I take the personal development classes—I get the little ones thinking about healthy eating and exercise and how they can get five a day, and how they can look after their teeth properly.'

It was the most he'd heard her say in one go, and she looked animated; clearly she loved her job and felt comfortable talking about it. 'So I take it you like your job?'

She smiled. 'I love it.'

Just as he loved his: something else they had in common. Tom paused, remembering what she'd said when he'd first walked in. 'I'm sorry about your parents.'

'And I'm sorry about your sister.' She bit her lip, looking awkward. 'I didn't know her very well, but she seemed nice.'

'She was. My big sister.' Tom sighed. 'And I feel worse because I was meant to go to France with her, Kevin and Joey to see our parents for New Year and I bailed out. Maybe if I'd been driving the crash wouldn't have happened.'

'You don't know that,' Flora said. 'And think of it another way—if you *had* been in the crash, Joey might've been left without anyone at all.'

'Mum and Dad would've stepped in to help, but they're nearly seventy now, and it's not fair to drag them back to England and make them run around after a little one. Dad's arthritis really gives him gyp.' He rubbed his hand across his forehead, but the tight band of tension refused to shift. 'I loved spending time with Joey when Susie was alive—I used to see them most weekends. I've always tried to be a good uncle and we used to have fun—but since the accident he's just put all these barriers up and I don't know how to get them down again.'

'Give it time,' she said again, her voice kind.

'Did he talk to you this afternoon?'

'A bit. He was a little shy.' She shrugged and looked away. 'But so am I, so that's OK.'

And that was one of the reasons why Flora seemed to

understand Joey better than he did: she knew what it was like to be shy, and Tom never had. And he couldn't help wondering what Flora was like when she wasn't shy. He knew she was practical and kind—but what did she look like when she laughed?

Or when she'd just been thoroughly kissed?

Oh, for pity's sake, he really needed to keep his libido under control.

Luckily his thoughts weren't showing on his face, because Flora continued, 'I read him some stories after we'd eaten—he chose them from the box I take to clinic—and then he fell asleep on the beanbag.'

'Bless him.' Tom bit his lip. 'I think he's had a better time with you than he would've done at the childminder's.' He sighed. 'I feel bad taking him to the childminder's for breakfast and then not picking him up until after dinner for half the week, but I work shifts—it's the only thing I can do. I was trying to avoid any more change in his life, but she told me the other week I'm going to have to find someone else because she's moving.'

'Would your childminder be Carol?' she asked.

Yet again, she'd surprised him. 'How did you know?'

'I know all the local childminders, through work,' Flora explained. 'Carol loves it here in Cornwall, but her husband's been promoted to his company's head office in London so that's why she has to move.'

'So if you know all the local childminders…' Tom brightened. 'Do you happen to know anyone with spare places who'd be good with Joey and could take him from half past six in the morning until school, and then after school until a quarter past seven or so? I can hardly take him with me to the station, in case we have a shout.'

'Nobody's got any spare places right now,' Flora said. 'The

ones who did have are already booked up from taking on Carol's clients. But I can ask around again, if you like.'

Yet another example of his failure at being a stand-in parent. 'Susie would've had that sorted out on day one,' Tom said grimly. 'When Carol told me she was leaving and I'd have to find someone else to look after Joey, I was still trying to get my head around what had happened and learning to fit my life round my nephew. I didn't have room in my head for anything else. And now I *wish* I'd made more of an effort.' He blew out a breath. 'Sorry. I shouldn't be dumping on you like this.'

'Not a problem. It's not going any further than me.'

'Trust you, you're a nurse?'

'Something like that.' Flora smiled at him, and Tom realised that she had dimples. Seriously cute dimples. Dimples he wanted to touch. Dimples he wanted to kiss.

Though now wasn't the time or the place. 'Thank you. You've been really kind. Can I impose on you and ask you what's your secret? You've got through to Joey when nobody else can, not even his teachers.'

She shrugged. 'I think he likes Banjo.'

The dog wagged his tail at hearing his name. The sound of Banjo's tail thumping the floor woke Joey, and he sat up, rubbing his eyes. For a moment, he stared wildly round him, as if not knowing where he was.

'Hey, Jojo, we're at Flora's. At the farm,' Tom said, going over to him and squatting down so that he was at his nephew's level. 'You fell asleep, sweetheart. I hear you've been running about with Banjo here and seeing the chickens and making brownies.'

Joey nodded.

'Did you have fun?'

Joey nodded again.

'That's good.' Tom smiled at him. 'The fire's out now so

your school's all safe again, ready for Monday morning. And we ought to let Flora get on. Shall we go home to Uncle Tom's upstairs house?'

Joey just looked at him.

Home.

Clearly Joey didn't think of Tom's flat as home. Maybe he should've moved into his sister's house instead of taking Joey back to his place, but he simply couldn't handle it. Every second he'd been in the house, he'd expected Susie to walk into the room at any time, and it had to be even harder for Joey. Right now, Tom was caught between the devil and the deep blue sea, and he hated himself for not being able to make Joey's world right again. For being a coward and escaping to work whenever he could, losing himself in the adrenalin rush of his job.

'Shall we say goodbye to Flora and Banjo?'

Joey yawned, then made a fuss of the dog, who licked him.

'You can come back any time you like and play with him,' Flora said. 'He liked playing ball with you this afternoon.'

Joey said nothing, but there was the ghost of a smile on his face.

'Thank you for having us,' Tom said, knowing that his nephew wasn't going to say it.

'My pleasure. Come back soon, Joey,' Flora said with a smile.

Tom tried slipping his hand into Joey's as they walked to the front door, but Joey twisted his hand away. Tom was careful not to let his feelings show on his face. 'Bye, Flora. Thanks again.'

He opened the car door, and Joey climbed onto his car seat. The little boy allowed Tom to fix the seatbelt, but Tom could see by the look on his nephew's face that Joey had retreated back into his shell again. He didn't even wave to Flora.

If only he could find a way of getting through to Joey.

He was just going to have to try harder.

CHAPTER THREE

DESPITE the fact that he'd lain awake half the night, worrying about Joey, Tom's body-clock was relentless. He didn't even need to look at his alarm to know that it was six o'clock. For pity's sake, it wasn't even light. And it was the weekend. Why couldn't he just turn over, stick the pillow over his head and go back to sleep?

Ha. He knew the answer to that. Because Joey woke early, too, and Tom needed to keep the little boy safe. His life had changed completely. Nowadays, he couldn't stay up until stupid o'clock watching films or playing online with his friends on a game console, or sleep in until midday on his day off. He had responsibilities.

Coffee, first. Tom dragged himself out of bed, then pulled on his dressing gown and headed for the kitchen. He blinked in surprise when he switched on the light and saw Joey sitting at the table in the dark, all dressed and ready to go out. Joey's long-sleeved T-shirt was on back to front and he was wearing odd socks; Tom couldn't help smiling. Cute beyond words. Part of him was tempted to ruffle his nephew's hair, but he knew that the little boy would only flinch away, so there was no point.

And that hurt.

'Why were you sitting in the dark, Jojo?' he asked gently.

Joey said nothing, but glanced over to the doorway.

Of course. He couldn't quite reach the light switch. Tom's flat wasn't designed for a four-year-old.

'I'll get a light put in here you *can* reach,' Tom promised. An uplighter would be the safest. Or maybe one on a timer switch. 'You look all ready to go out.'

Joey nodded.

'Where do you want to go?' And please don't let him say 'home', Tom begged silently.

'I want to play with Banjo.'

Flora's dog had clearly made the breakthrough that none of the adults had been able to make, because this was the longest sentence that Joey had strung together since the accident.

It would be an imposition on Flora, Tom knew, but this was the most animated he'd seen Joey since the little boy had come to live with him. He couldn't afford to let the opportunity slip away. Though going to visit Flora at this time of the morning would be a little too much to ask; he needed some delaying tactics.

'OK, sweetheart, we'll go and see Banjo.' *And Flora.* Awareness prickled all the way down Tom's spine, and he squashed it ruthlessly. This wasn't about his attraction to the sweet, gentle school nurse who had the most kissable mouth he'd ever seen. This was about his nephew. 'But it's a bit early to go and visit anyone just yet; it's still dark outside. I'm not even dressed—and I don't know about you, but I really could do with some breakfast first. How about we make something to eat, then go and buy some flowers to say thank you to Flora for looking after you yesterday, and a...' What did you buy dogs? Tom's parents had always had cats rather than dogs, and he hadn't had the space in his life to look after an animal properly so he had no pets. 'A ball or something for Banjo?' he finished.

Joey nodded.

Tom put water in the kettle and switched it on. 'What do you want for breakfast?'

Joey shrugged.

'Juice? Cereals?' Flora had got through to him yesterday by baking. Tom didn't bake. He did the bare minimum when it came to cooking: stir-fries, pasta and baked potatoes were pretty much his limit. Anyway, suggesting cake for breakfast wasn't exactly healthy.

But there had to be something they could do.

'How about a bacon sandwich?' he asked. 'We can make it as a team. How about you're the chef, in charge of buttering the bread and squirting on the tomato ketchup, and I'll grill the bacon?'

Joey gave him a tiny smile, and went to the drawer where Tom kept the tea-towels. Without a word, he tucked a tea-towel round himself like an apron, the way he had in the photo Flora had shown Tom the previous evening, then fetched the butter and tomato ketchup from the fridge.

This was good, Tom thought. A positive step.

Joey buttered the bread while Tom grilled the bacon. Tom carefully laid the cooked bacon on the bread, then looked at Joey. 'Over to you, Chef.'

Joey squeezed tomato ketchup over the bacon—a bit too much for Tom's taste, but he'd wash it down with coffee and a smile because no way was he going to reject his nephew's efforts. 'Excellent teamwork. High five, Chef.' He lifted his palm, hoping that Joey would respond.

For a moment, he didn't think Joey was going to react— and then Joey smiled and touched his palm to Tom's. Only momentarily, but in Tom's view it was huge progress from the way things had been. And it gave him hope for the future.

'Can we see Banjo now?' Joey asked when they'd finished, his face eager.

'Once you've washed your face and changed your shirt—

because they're both covered in ketchup—and cleaned your teeth,' Tom said. 'And I need to wash up the breakfast things. Then we'll go to the shop on the way.'

'My singing isn't that bad, you horrible dog,' Flora said, laughing as Banjo started barking.

But then he went over to the kitchen door and barked again.

'Visitors?' Odd. She wasn't expecting anyone, and it was too early for the postman. But there was no other reason why her dog would be barking by the front door. She switched off the vacuum cleaner and went to answer the door.

'Oh—Tom and Joey! Hello.' She hadn't expected to see them today, despite telling them the previous evening that they could come round at any time. And it was incredibly early. Barely after breakfast.

'We wanted to bring you something—didn't we, Jojo?' Tom said.

Joey nodded, all wide-eyed.

'These are for you.' Tom handed her the biggest bunch of flowers she'd ever seen. 'We weren't sure what colour you like, but Joey thinks all girls like pink.'

And there was every shade of pink. Bold cerise gerberas, tiny pale pink spray carnations, even some blush-pink roses.

Flora couldn't remember anyone ever buying her flowers before—except her parents, on her birthday and when she'd qualified as a nurse—and it flustered her. 'I, um…' She felt the betraying tide of colour sweep into her cheeks. 'Um, they're lovely. I, um…' Oh, help. 'Do you want to come in?'

'This is for Banjo.' Joey was carrying what Flora recognised as a squeaky toy bone.

'Thank you. He loves those.'

Just to prove it, when Joey squeaked the bone, Banjo

bounced into the middle of the room, bowing down and wagging his tail to signal that he was ready to play.

Be practical, Flora told herself. Don't make an idiot of yourself. 'I'll put these lovely flowers in water,' she said. 'Would you like a coffee?'

'I'd love one.' Tom smiled at her, and she felt her toes curl. Which was crazy. She didn't react to people like that. Anyway, he wasn't here to see her…was he?

To cover her confusion, she turned to the little boy. 'Joey, would you like some milk or some juice?'

Joey shook his head and continued playing with the dog.

Tom glanced at the vacuum cleaner. 'Sorry, you were busy.'

'It's OK. I was only vacuuming. And you brought me those gorgeous flowers.'

'It was the least we could do. You were a total star yesterday. We wanted to say thank you.'

He'd brought her flowers to say thanks for helping with Joey. No other reason. She squished the ridiculous hope that he'd bought them for the usual reason a man bought a woman flowers. Of course not. She already knew she wasn't the kind of woman who could make men look twice; she was way too short, thirty pounds too heavy, and on the rare occasion she wore a skirt it was usually six inches below the knee rather than six inches above. Plus she spent most of her time with a red face, tongue-tied. No way would someone like Tom be interested in her.

As always when faced with a social situation involving adults, she took refuge in practicalities, gesturing to Tom to sit at the scrubbed pine table in the centre of the kitchen, then busying herself arranging the flowers in a vase. Once she'd put them on the table, she made two mugs of coffee, took the remaining brownies from the tin and put them on a plate, then sat down with Tom and slid the plate across to him. 'Help yourself.'

'Thanks…' he smiled at her '…but, lovely as those brownies are, I'd better pass. We've just had breakfast. Chef Joey there makes a mean bacon sandwich.'

She raised an eyebrow. 'I assume you grilled the bacon.'

'But he did the important bit—he buttered the bread and added the tomato sauce.'

Joey clearly wasn't paying attention to anyone else except Banjo, but then Tom lowered his voice. 'I'm sorry we turned up unannounced. He told me this morning that he wanted to come and play with Banjo—and it's the longest sentence he's said in a month. I feel bad about taking up your spare time, but this was a chance to get through to him. I just couldn't turn it down.'

'It's not a problem,' Flora said, keeping her voice equally low. 'I wasn't doing anything in particular, just the usual Saturday chores.'

'I don't want to make things awkward with your boyfriend.'

She felt the betraying colour heat her cheeks again. 'I don't have a boyfriend.' The boys at school had never looked twice at her, she'd never been the partying type as a student nurse, and she knew that she wouldn't even be on the radar of a gorgeous firefighter like Tom Nicholson. Then a really nasty thought hit her. 'Is it going to be a problem for your girlfriend, Joey coming here to play with Banjo?'

'There's nobody serious in my life—just Joey.' He smiled wryly. 'Let's just say my last girlfriend found it a bit hard to share my time. The way she saw it, I should've made my parents come back to England to look after him.'

'How selfish of h—' Flora clapped a hand to her mouth. 'Sorry, it's not my place to judge.'

'No, you got it right first time. And she told me that the day after the accident.' For a moment, he looked grim. 'Apart from the fact that we hadn't been dating for very long, it wasn't a hard choice to make. Joey comes first.'

'Well, of course he does.'

Tom gave her an approving smile that made her feel as if she were glowing from the inside.

'I've been thinking about your childminder issue. I could help out, if you like.' The words tumbled out before Flora could stop them. 'I finish at five, the same time as the after-school club—so I could meet him from there if you like. There's only me and Banjo to please ourselves, and it's as easy to cook for two as it is for one, so if you're out on a shout or something he can have his tea here with me—if you think he'd like that,' she added swiftly.

Tom looked surprised at her offer. 'That's really kind of you,' he said carefully.

Oh, no. He'd obviously taken it the wrong way. She'd better explain. 'Look, I just know what it's like to lose both parents,' she said. 'And that wasn't me trying to—well, you know.' She blushed again.

Trying to come on to him? From another woman, Tom wouldn't have been so sure. But with Flora, he knew she was genuine; he hadn't known her long, but it was obvious that she was the type to wear her heart on her sleeve. She was offering to help because she was kind, because she cared, because she'd lost her own parents and she could understand exactly how Joey felt—and she wasn't emotionally hopeless with the boy, the way he was.

'I know it was a genuine offer,' he said softly, 'and I'm not trying to come on to you, either.' Though he knew that wasn't strictly true. He couldn't put his finger on it, but something about Flora Loveday drew him. And it was completely unex-pected because she was nothing like the women he usually dated. She wasn't sophisticated, fashionable or glamorous. But there really was something about her that made him—well, just *want* her.

Though, right now, he knew he couldn't think about dating anyone. His life was too complicated. He pulled himself together. 'It's always good to make a new friend. Especially one as kind as you.'

She blushed even more, and Tom couldn't help smiling. Flora was so sweet. And there was a vulnerability about her that made him feel protective. Strong.

'And it's really all right for you to help me with Joey?'

'I wouldn't have offered if I didn't mean it.'

Tom closed his eyes for a moment. It seemed as if his prayers had all been answered. 'Flora, thank you. I have no idea what I would've done if you hadn't offered to help.'

Looking embarrassed, she glanced away. 'It's not a big deal. Joey's a nice little boy. But he might not want to come here.'

Tom smiled. 'Considering that he was up before I was, this morning—and I always wake at six—and he'd got himself dressed, with odd socks and his shirt on back to front, ready to come and see you and play with Banjo…I think he's going to say yes. But you're right—we do need to ask him first.' He looked over to where his nephew was busy making a fuss of Banjo, rubbing the dog's tummy while the spaniel had his eyes closed in bliss.

'Joey—can you come here a moment, sweetheart, please?'

Joey eyed the dog, clearly torn between making a fuss of him and doing what his uncle had asked, but eventually trotted over.

'How would you feel about Flora picking you up from after-school club in future?' Tom asked.

Joey frowned. 'Carol picks me up from school.'

'I know, but Carol has to go to live in London very soon,' Tom said gently. 'It's a big change for you, I know, but I've been trying to find someone you'd like to stay with while I'm at work.'

Joey's hazel eyes turned thoughtful. 'Would Banjo come, too?'

'Banjo's normally here during the day,' Flora said. 'But he'd be here to meet you when we got back from school. You could help me take him for a walk. Would you like that?'

Joey considered it, then nodded shyly.

'And then I'll come and fetch you as soon as I've finished work,' Tom said.

'Can I play with Banjo again now?'

Tom smiled. 'Sure.'

Joey raced back to the dog and found the squeaky bone.

'When do you want me to start picking him up?' Flora asked.

Tom thought about it. 'Carol's right in the middle of packing everything now. It's pretty disruptive for Joey, and I'm trying to keep things as calm as I can.' Calm and relaxed, like it was here at the farmhouse, Tom thought. Everything was neat and tidy, though it wasn't the kind of house where you'd be scared to move a cushion out of place. It was more that everything felt *right* just where it was, warm and welcoming and organised and comfortable. Just what Joey needed.

As for what Tom himself needed…he wasn't going to examine that too closely.

'I've got a day off on Monday. I don't have anything planned, so I could start then, if you like?' Flora suggested.

'Actually, I'm off myself on Monday and Tuesday—I work four days on and then four days off,' he said. 'But if you can do Wednesday to Friday this week, that'd be brilliant.'

'What time does your shift start?'

'I work seven until seven.'

'So what happens in the mornings,' she asked, 'if you have

to be at work at seven and school doesn't start until a quarter to nine?'

'I'm still working on that,' Tom admitted. 'I've been dropping him at Carol's at half past six.'

She shrugged. 'Well—I don't start work until nine, so you can do that with me, too. I'll have plenty of time to take him to school on the days you're at work.'

Tom stared at her. 'Really?' Usually, if something was too good to be true, it usually was. It couldn't be possible to sort out his hours and Joey's so easily—could it? 'Half past six is really OK with you?'

She smiled. 'I'm used to being up with the chickens, even though I don't have to feed them myself any more. And it'll be nice to have breakfast with someone in the mornings.'

She was so calm about it, so serene. Did she know what an angel she was? Tom wanted to hug her, but he had a feeling that she'd find it as awkward as Joey did. Something told him that Flora wasn't used to people hugging her. Except maybe some of her younger patients—he'd already noticed that she had children's drawings stuck to the door of her fridge with magnets.

'I'll need your contact numbers. And you'll also need to tell the school,' Flora added.

'Sure. If you have a piece of paper and a pen, I'll write my numbers down for you.'

Flora handed him her mobile phone. 'Better still, you could put them straight in there.'

Her fingers brushed against his and a wave of awareness swept down his spine. Not that he'd dare act on that awareness. Apart from the fact that she was shy—with him, not with Joey—if he messed this up, he'd lose a friend as well as help that he badly needed right now. He needed to keep a lid on this. Trying not to think about how soft her skin was and wondering how it would feel against his mouth, he keyed in his home number, his mobile and the number of the fire station. 'I've already got your numbers. I assume if I need to get you at work I should ring the surgery?'

'Yes, or try my mobile—I don't answer if I'm driving, though, so it'll go through to voicemail,' she warned.

'Good—that's sensible. I've had to cut too many people out of cars when they've been trying to talk on the phone and drive at the same time. Why they couldn't just pull over and make the call safely, or use a headset…' He rolled his eyes. 'Sorry. Preaching to the converted. And, as a medic, you know all that already.'

Flora smiled. 'Yes.'

She went quiet and shy on him again once they'd finished with the practicalities, but Tom was aware that he was eking out his coffee, putting off the moment when he'd have to leave here. Scared of being on his own with his nephew and failing to connect with him yet again? Or something else? He didn't want to analyse that too closely. And this really wasn't fair to Flora, taking up her day. 'Come on, Joey. Remember we said we'd go and play football in the park?'

'Can Banjo come?' Joey asked.

'No, Flora has things to do,' Tom said, before Joey could suggest taking up even more of Flora's time.

'Can we come back tomorrow?'

Tom was searching for an excuse when Flora said, 'I don't mind. I don't have anything much planned.'

'Tell you what, maybe Joey and I can take you out to lunch.' The words were out before he could stop them and he could see the surprise on her face—and the wariness. Help. He needed to take this down a notch. Make it clear that he was inviting her out with both of them, not on a proper date.

Though he was horribly aware that he'd like to have lunch with Flora on her own and get to know her better—a lot better.

'I mean, you fed us on Friday so it's our turn to feed you—right, Jojo?'

Joey nodded.

'And I know a place that does a really good Sunday roast, just down the road from here.' Tom smiled at her. 'So, can we take you to lunch tomorrow?'

'That'd be lovely. Thank you.'

'Great. We'll pick you up at half past eleven.'

It wasn't a proper date, Flora told herself as she stood in the doorway, waving as Tom's car headed down the driveway. They were just acquaintances who were on their way to becoming friends. Nothing more than that.

And she'd better not let herself forget it.

CHAPTER FOUR

DESPITE her resolutions to be calm and sensible, Flora found herself changing her outfit three times the next morning. She really should've asked Tom whether she needed to dress up for lunch.

Then again, they were going out with Joey, so the restaurant was more likely to be a family-friendly place. Which meant smart-casual rather than trendy—and besides, she didn't do trendy clothes. In the end, cross with herself for minding, she opted for a pair of smart black trousers, a long-sleeved cerise T-shirt and low-heeled sensible shoes. Hopefully this would strike the right balance.

She was relieved when Tom turned up wearing black chinos and a light sweater. And she suppressed the thought that he looked utterly gorgeous, like a model. He was her *friend*. Right?

Joey's seat was in the back of the car, but she noticed that Tom included Joey in the conversation, even though the little boy barely answered much above yes, no and—from what she could see in the rear-view mirror—a shrug.

Lunch was as excellent as Tom had promised. Flora noted that Tom helped Joey cut up his meat without making a big deal about it, just a soft, 'Can I give you a hand with that, sweetheart?' Tom really was a natural father figure, even though he clearly didn't think he was good enough. And they all had fun with the ice-cream machine; Tom helped Joey make a huge mountain in his bowl, and the little boy looked really happy as he added sprinkles and sauces from the toppings bar. He decorated Flora's and Tom's ice cream, too.

'That,' Flora said, 'is the best sundae I've ever seen.' She smiled at the little boy. 'Thank you, Joey. I'm really going to enjoy this.'

'Me, too,' Tom said. 'You're really good at decorating ice cream, Jojo.'

Joey's smile said it all for him: right now, all was right with his world.

Flora exchanged a glance with Tom, and her heart did another flip. This felt like being part of a family. And the scary thing was that she liked it. A lot.

'I think,' Tom said solemnly, patting his stomach afterwards, 'we need to walk off all that ice cream. It's really sunny outside, so how about we go to the park?'

Joey nodded, and Tom drove them there. Even though it was a chilly February afternoon, there were plenty of people walking through the gardens, pushing a pram or with a toddler running on the grass beside them. At the far end of the park, there was a playground with swings, slides and climbing frames; even from this distance, Flora could see that it was busy.

'Hello, Flora! Fancy seeing you here.' Jenny Walters smiled at her; she glanced at Tom and Joey and her smile turned speculative. 'Out to the park for the afternoon?'

'I, um. Yes.' Flora felt colour bursting into her face. Oh, no. The last thing they needed was gossip. But how could she explain that she and Tom were just friends, without it sounding like a cover story? 'You, too?' she asked, hoping that it would distract Jenny.

'Just me and Rachel. Damien's at home watching the football.' Jenny glanced at her daughter, who was holding her hand. 'Actually, I'm glad I've caught you. I know I'm probably worrying about nothing, but Rachel's got this thing on her foot and I don't like the look of it.' She bit her lip. 'Sorry, I can see you're out with your...' she paused '...*friend*, and I know I shouldn't ask outside clinic or the surgery.'

But it would only take a moment and would stop her worrying. And Flora always felt more comfortable when she was doing something practical. At work, she wasn't shy because she knew who she was: Flora Loveday, nurse. Plus looking at Rachel's foot might take Jenny's mind off the fact that she was accompanying Tom and Joey. She glanced at Tom and Joey. 'Would you mind if I took a look? I'll only be a couple of minutes.'

'No, that's fine—isn't it, Jojo?' Tom said.

Joey nodded solemnly.

'Thanks.' Flora smiled at them. 'Jenny, would you and Rachel like to come and sit down on that bench over there? Then, if you don't mind taking your shoe off, Rachel, I'll have a swift look at your foot.'

'It looks like grains of pepper on the bottom of her foot,' Jenny said. 'I thought it was maybe a splinter but she hasn't been running around barefoot in the garden, not at this time of year. I've tried putting mag sulph paste on it with a plaster on top, just in case it was a splinter, but nothing happened.'

From the description, Flora had a pretty good idea what it was, but she needed to see it for herself, just to be sure. 'Wow, that's a nice sock, Rachel,' she said as the little girl took her shoe off to reveal a bright pink sock with black pawprints. 'Those are pawprints just like my Banjo makes.'

'I like dogs,' Rachel said. 'What sort is yours?'

'He's a springer spaniel, and he lives up to his name because he bounces about everywhere,' Flora said with a grin. 'Guess what colour he is?'

'Black and white?'

'Half-right. Guess again.' Flora kept the little girl distracted by chatting while she inspected her foot.

'Brown and white?'

'Absolutely. Hey, do you know a song about a farmer's dog that almost sounds like Banjo?' she asked.

Just as she'd hoped, Rachel began singing, 'There was a farmer had a dog…'

And, to her surprise, when Rachel got to the bit where a letter in the dog's name was replaced by a clap, Joey joined in.

Tom looked transfixed. And, even though she'd seen enough to have her suspicions confirmed, Flora let Rachel and Joey finish the song before she asked her next question.

'That was brilliant singing, Rachel—and brilliant clapping, Joey.'

Both children looked pleased.

'You can sing us another clapping song, if you like,' Flora said. 'But first—Rachel, does it hurt when you walk?'

'A bit,' Rachel said. 'It's prickly.'

'OK. Well, the good news is, we can do something about that. Sing me another song, and I'll have a quick word with Mummy.' She smiled at the little boy. 'Joey, can you help Rachel with the clapping bits?'

Rachel was clearly delighted to have a younger child join in and, while she explained to Joey what they needed to do, Flora explained to Jenny what the problem was.

'It's a verruca,' she said.

'But I thought that was like a single big black spot?'

'Sometimes you get a cluster together, like this one,' Flora said. 'It's actually a wart on the bottom of the foot, so you might hear it called a plantar wart. Because of where it is, it gets trodden into the foot, so that's why it looks like spots rather than a growth. It's really common and nothing to worry about; my guess is, she picked it up at swimming.'

'I had a verruca when I was a kid,' Jenny said. 'I remember my mum taking me to the hospital, and this woman put a thing on my foot that burned and really hurt—and she told me off for making a fuss.'

Flora curled her lip in disgust. 'That's awful! You can still do the freezing treatment, but you can get something at the pharmacy so you can do it at home, and it's a special liquid so it shouldn't hurt. Or you can try duct tape.'

'Duct tape?' Jenny looked surprised.

'It works fairly well, but it's a little bit more long-winded. What you need to do is cut the tape just to the size of the verruca and put it on—it stops air getting to the skin and so it dies off and lets you get to the verruca,' Flora explained. 'Keep it on for six days, then take the tape off, soak Rachel's foot in a bowl of warm water for five minutes, then dry it and rub the area with a pumice stone to get rid of the dead skin. Then you put more duct tape on, and keep following the cycle. Usually it goes in three or four weeks.'

'I'll try that,' Jenny said.

'It's really infectious, so make sure you don't share towels,' Flora warned.

'And I'd better stop taking her swimming for a while.'

'Nowadays, the advice is just to cover it with waterproof plaster when you're swimming and use flip-flops in the communal areas,' Flora said with a smile.

Just when she'd finished explaining, Rachel and Joey sang and clapped the last bit of their song.

'That was brilliant, Rachel and Joey.' Flora applauded them both. 'Rachel, I've told Mummy what she needs to do, and you'll be pleased to know it won't hurt and you can still go swimming.'

The little girl beamed. 'Yay!'

'We'd better let you get on. Sorry we interrupted.' Jenny

gave Tom an apologetic smile, then patted Flora's shoulder. 'Thanks, Flora. You're such a star.'

Absolutely right, Tom thought, though he noticed how Flora shrugged the praise aside.

'Sorry about that, Tom,' Flora said as they headed towards the playground again.

'No, you're fine. I guess that's one of the perils of being a medic—everyone always wants to stop and ask your advice instead of going to the surgery.'

'I don't mind,' she said.

No, he thought, because she was special. She made a real difference to people's lives. 'Actually, that was fascinating. I learned a lot from that.' As well as reinforcing what he'd already guessed: that Flora was patient, was instinctively brilliant with children, and was great at reassuring worried parents, too. And he'd noticed that, even though Flora clearly knew Rachel's mum, she'd been shy with the woman until she'd actually been treating the child: and then the professional nurse had taken over, pushing the shyness away. Flora clearly had confidence in herself at work, but none outside. And he really couldn't understand why. Not wanting her to go back into her shell, he kept her talking about work. 'I had no idea about verrucas. I can't remember having one as a kid.'

'You must've been about the only child who didn't get one,' she said with a grin. 'Does Joey like swimming?'

He had no idea. 'Susie used to have a paddling pool for him in the garden, but I don't know if he ever went to a proper pool or had lessons. Probably not, or the swimming teacher would've got in touch with me by now, through Carol or something.' He sighed. 'I doubt if Joey will tell me himself, so I'll have to ask Matty Roper.'

'It might help you get a routine going, if you do things together on certain days—well, obviously depending on your shift,' she said. 'Maybe your first day off after a shift, you could go swimming together. And putting stickers on a calendar will help him remember what you're doing and when—that might make him feel a bit more secure with you.'

'I would never have thought of that.' Tom said. 'You're a genius.'

She shrugged. 'I'm no genius. I work with children, so I pick things up from the teachers and childminders.'

Hiding her light under a bushel again, Tom thought. Why did she do that? Why was she so uncomfortable with praise? Had her parents been the sort who were never satisfied and kept pushing? Or was it something else?

They reached the playground, and Joey made a beeline for the swing.

'Shall I push you?' Tom asked.

Joey shook his head, and proved that he could manage on his own.

Flora was sitting on the bench near the swings where she could watch; feeling useless, Tom joined her.

'OK?' she asked.

'Sure,' he lied. Hell. He needed distraction. And Flora was really, really good at being distracting.

Not that he would ruin things by telling her that there were amber flecks in her brown eyes. Or that her mouth was a perfect rosebud.

Pushing the thoughts away, he said, 'Did you always want to be a nurse?'

'I wanted to be a vet when I was small, and I was always bandaging up the dogs and the cats,' Flora said.

He could just imagine it, and couldn't help smiling.

'But I knew I wouldn't be able to handle putting animals to sleep, and Dad said I was so soft-hearted I'd end up taking in every stray brought in for surgery and I'd have to buy a

thousand acres to house them all—and he was probably right,'
Flora finished with a smile.

'But the medic part of it stuck?' he asked.

She nodded. 'I was going to take my exams to be a children's nurse when I'd qualified, and work at St Piran's.'

'So why didn't you?'

She shrugged. 'I realised Mum and Dad were struggling a
bit. I couldn't just leave them to it, so I came home to look after
them and did some agency work. The job as school liaison
nurse came through last year—ironically, not long after Mum
died. She would've been so pleased.'

'Was she a nurse, too?'

Flora shook her head. 'She and Dad, their life was the farm.
Loveday's Organics. Dad believed in it well before it became
trendy, and he worked with the Trevelyans on sorting out a veg
box scheme. Though I didn't really want to take the farm over
when I left school.' She gave a wry laugh. 'Whoever heard of
a farm girl being scared of chickens?'

'You're scared of chickens?' Tom asked.

'Not any more, but I was for years, even as a teen.' She
blushed prettily again, and Tom had to stop himself leaning
over to steal a kiss from that beautiful rosebud mouth. Did
Flora really have no idea how lovely she was?

'I think they knew I was nervous and it made them nervous, too, so it made them flap more. And that in turn made
me more nervous, and it just got worse. Nowadays, it's not so
bad. Toby taught me how to keep them calm, and I can even
go in and collect eggs now.'

Tom was surprised to feel a flicker of jealousy at the other
man's name. She'd said she didn't have a boyfriend... 'Who's
Toby?'

'He manages the farm for me. He's worked with us for the
last four years—he was Dad's assistant, but I know he took
as much as he could off Dad's shoulders. His wife's a real

sweetie, too. Their little boy's a couple of years older than Joey.' She looked thoughtful. 'Actually, they live in the cottage at the bottom of the driveway. It might be nice for Max and Joey to play together.'

'Maybe.' Tom was even crosser with himself for being pleased that Toby was clearly committed elsewhere. He had no right to be jealous and no right to dictate who Flora saw. 'Though Joey doesn't make friends very easily. He keeps himself to himself.'

'Max is a nice little boy. He'd be kind. Maybe we could do a play-date in a couple of weeks, when Joey's used to me and has settled in.' As if she could sense the knot of worry in his stomach and wanted to head him off the subject, she said, 'So what about you—did you always want to be a firefighter?'

'No, I was going to be an arctic explorer or drive a racing car.'

She laughed. 'So it was always going to be something dangerous, then?'

'Sort of.' He sighed. 'I think Dad was always a bit disappointed that I didn't go to university, but I'm taking my firefighter exams and I'm ready to move up to the next level, so I've proved to him that it's a career and not just a whim.'

'So what made you decide to be a firefighter?'

He could lie and give an anodyne response, but he had a feeling that Flora would know. And she deserved better than that. He took a deep breath. 'My best friend at school died in a house fire when I was thirteen.'

She winced. 'Sorry. That must've been hard for you.'

His world had been blown wide apart. Until then, it had never occurred to him that people his own age could die. Stupid, because of course they could. But he'd never known anyone die who wasn't really, really old and really, really sick. 'Yes. I found it pretty hard to deal with. And I couldn't help thinking, if I'd been a grown-up, one of the firefighters,

I would've been able to save Ben.' He shrugged. 'I know the fire wasn't my fault, but I guess becoming a firefighter was my way of trying to make up for what happened to him.' He'd never actually told anyone that before; he risked a glance at Flora, and to his surprise she wasn't looking at him as if he was crazy. She actually seemed to understand. 'Ben's the reason why I almost never lose anyone.' Why he drove himself past every barrier, no matter how scary. 'I remember how hard it was for his parents, when he died, and I don't want anyone else to go through that.'

'It takes someone very special to be that dedicated,' she said softly.

He shrugged. 'I've done the work for long enough to have a fair idea what I'm doing when it comes to fires, even though they can be unpredictable.' He probably took more risks than others, but he didn't really have a family at home to worry about.

Until now.

And that was a real struggle. He'd been thinking about his job, whether he ought to change to something with more child-friendly hours and less danger so he could protect Joey. Yet, at the same time, being a firefighter was all he'd ever wanted to do. He couldn't imagine doing anything else. And he found it hard to be a stand-in father; work was an escape for him. Which, he thought wryly, made him a really awful person. 'But being a parent to Joey…that's something I don't think I'll ever be able to get right,' he admitted.

'Probably because you're trying too hard.'

He frowned. 'How do you mean?'

'It's impossible to be the perfect parent,' she said gently. 'I see new mums breaking their hearts because they can't get it right and everyone else seems to get their babies to sleep and eat much more easily than they can. But then they come to realise that you can't be perfect and your best really is good enough. And that takes the pressure off and stops them trying so hard, and then the babies relax too and it all works out.' She took his hand and squeezed it. 'And it's even harder when you're suddenly dropped into a parenting role—when you're expecting a baby you have a few months to get used to the idea, and your confidence grows as the baby does. Joey's four, already thinking and acting for himself, and you just need to give yourself a bit of time to catch up with him.'

He thought about it.

And, to his shock, he realised that she was right. He *was* trying too hard. Trying to make up for Susie and Kevin not being there any more, trying to be the perfect stand-in and getting frustrated with himself and Joey because the barriers between them seemed to grow every day; and then feeling guilty because he'd escaped into work to forget his problems outside.

'You're a very wise woman, Flora Loveday.'

She just smiled.

They sat in a companionable silence, watching Joey on the swings, until they heard a scream. They turned round to see a woman cradling her child on the ground by the climbing frame.

'That's Maisie Phillipson and Barney,' Flora said. 'Tom, would you mind if—?'

'Go,' he cut in softly, knowing exactly what she was going to ask. He was beginning to realise that Flora just couldn't stand by and do nothing if there was a crisis and she knew she could do something to help. And he recognised that this was her way of dealing with her shyness, too; doing practical things meant that she didn't have time to think about what was going on and to feel self-conscious.

'Maisie, what happened?' Flora asked as she reached the climbing frame.

'One minute, Barney was climbing—the next, he was on

the ground.' Maisie bit her lip. 'I should've been watching him, not chatting.'

'Even if you'd watched him for every second, you wouldn't have been able to catch him,' Flora said. 'Do you want me to take a look at him?'

'Flora, you're an angel. Yes, please,' Maisie said, giving her a grateful smile.

Flora sat on the sand next to the little boy. 'Hi, there, Barney. Mummy says you fell off the climbing frame. Does anything hurt?'

'No-o.' Barney looked torn between braving it out and showing just what a tough six-year-old he was and bursting into tears.

'That's quite a big fall, and you're being really brave,' Flora said with a smile. 'Did you hit your head at all?'

'I think so.'

'Did everything go black after you hit your head?'

'No.'

That was a good sign. 'Can I just look into your eyes with my special torch?' Flora asked.

'All right.'

She took the torch from her handbag. Both of Barney's pupils were equal and reactive, to her relief. 'Righty. And now I need you to do something else for me.' She took a thimble with a bee on it from her handbag and slipped it onto her forefinger. 'Can you follow the bee with your eyes?'

He did so, and she checked his eye movements as she moved the bee from side to side.

'That's brilliant. I haven't got a sticker on me, but I'll bring you one when I'm in school next week,' she promised.

Barney looked hopeful. 'Can it be a rocket sticker?'

'Absolutely a rocket sticker,' she said, smiling back.

'Can I go and play now?'

Maisie sighed. 'All right. But *not* on the climbing frame. And be careful!'

'He'll be fine, Maisie,' Flora reassured her. 'You can give him some infant paracetamol when you get home, if he says anything hurts, and just keep an eye on him. If he still has a headache in six hours' time, or he's sick or passes out, or he feels really dizzy or can't see properly, or goes to sleep and you can't wake him, then take him straight to hospital.' She smiled ruefully. 'I really ought to keep a bumped-head leaflet in my handbag.'

After saying goodbye to Maisie, she returned to Tom.

'Everything OK?' Tom asked, standing up as she neared the bench.

'Bumped head. He'll be fine.'

'You must see that all the time.'

'Pretty much every session at the primary school,' she agreed with a smile. 'I know the advice off by heart.'

They walked over to the swings; Joey had slowed down and was just letting the ropes rock him back and forth.

'Shall we go down the slide, Jojo?' Tom asked.

The little boy shook his head. Before Tom could ask anything else, he slid off the seat and headed for the seats on a spring. He chose the one like a frog, and sat bouncing on it with his shoulders hunched and his back turned to Tom.

'Are you OK?' Flora asked.

'Yes.'

She could see on his face that he wasn't. And she knew that male pride would get in the way of him telling her what was wrong. But he'd confided in her earlier about his best friend as a child, and something in his eyes had told her that it wasn't something that most people knew about. She was pretty sure that it was the same as whatever was upsetting him now; but he needed to get this out in the open to let him deal with it. Which meant pushing beyond her own boundaries, not letting her shyness get in the way of helping him. She took a deep breath. 'Don't fib.'

Tom sighed. 'I guess no, then.'

And now for the biggie. She forced herself to say it. 'Want to tell me about it?'

He was silent for so long that she thought she'd gone too far. And then he bit his lip. 'Joey used to love the slide. On Sunday mornings, if Susie was cooking Sunday lunch for us, Kev and I used to take Joey to the park for a kickabout with a football, and we always ended up on the slides and the swings afterwards. He used to love going down the slide, sitting on my lap or his dad's, when he was really tiny.'

And she could see on Tom's face how much he missed it. And how hurt he was that his nephew didn't want to do that any more; what he could see was Joey's rejection, not the scared little boy behind it.

'He's probably remembering that, too, and it probably makes him miss his parents, but he just doesn't know how to tell you,' Flora said softly, taking Tom's hand and squeezing it. 'It might even be that he's scared to tell you, in case you're upset too.'

'Upset with him?'

She shook her head. 'Grieving. Missing his parents the way he does. I can remember my grandmother dying when I was about four, and my mum crying, and I felt helpless because I didn't know how to make things better for her. And because I felt helpless, I hid in my room and avoided her until she'd stopped crying and she was Mum again. I wasn't rejecting her—I just didn't know how to deal with it.'

He returned the pressure of her fingers and didn't drop her hand. 'You're right, and it's stupid of me to feel rejected because he doesn't want to go on the slide with me.' He swallowed hard. 'It's just that now he hates being touched. I can't even give him a hug or ruffle his hair because he really doesn't like it—he pulls away every time. He never used to hate it. He loved playing rough-and-tumble games with me and his dad. He used to run to me and give me a huge, huge hug hello whenever he saw me. And now…' Tom shook his head. 'He's quiet and still and…I just can't reach him.'

'It's a hard situation for both of you, Tom,' she said gently. 'Give yourself a break. You're doing your best.'

'And it's not good enough. I don't know how to be a dad.'

Flora had the strongest feeling that Tom hated failing at anything, but this was even harder because he loved the little boy and wanted to make Joey's world all right again.

'You're doing better than you think you are,' she told him. 'You spend time with him, you talk to him, you take him out—that's a lot more than some kids get from their parents.'

'I guess so.' Tom looked haunted. 'I just wish…'

'Wish what?' she prompted.

He shook his head. 'Never mind.'

Obviously he felt he'd already let his guard down too much with her. But Flora also noticed that he was still holding her hand. Taking comfort from her.

Well, it was what a friend would do. Slightly less ostentatious than a public hug. And, if it made him feel better, she was perfectly happy to hold his hand.

As for the awareness flickering down her spine, the tingling in her skin—well, she'd just have to ignore it. This wasn't about them. It was about Joey.

Eventually Joey stopped bouncing on the frog seat.

'Shall we go and have a hot chocolate to warm us up?' Tom suggested.

Joey nodded. Although he didn't hold his uncle's hand, he did at least fall into step beside him; and Flora noticed that Tom shortened his stride to make it easier for the little boy to keep up. He was sensitive to the needs of others and she liked that. A lot.

When they'd finished their hot chocolates—which Tom insisted on paying for—he drove them back to the farmhouse.

'We'd better let you get on,' Tom said, before she had the chance to invite them in.

'OK. Well, thanks for lunch. I really enjoyed that—and the park.' She smiled at Joey. 'Uncle Tom has a day off on Monday and Tuesday, so he's going to pick you up from school. But I'll see you on Wednesday for breakfast, and after school we'll take Banjo for a walk and collect some eggs, yes?'

Joey nodded.

'Thanks, Flora. You're a gem,' Tom said softly. 'We'll see you on Wednesday.'

CHAPTER FIVE

'FLORA?'

Even without the caller display showing the number on her phone, she would've recognised Tom's deep voice.

'Yes?'

'Are you busy right now?'

'I was about to go out,' she admitted.

'Never mind, then. I'll catch you later.'

'Tom?' She paused. Why would he be phoning her mid-morning? 'Is everything OK? I mean, have you been called in to work? Do you need me to pick up Joey?'

'No—nothing like that. But I did want to talk to you about Joey.'

He needed her. And somehow that made it a lot easier for her to push the hated shyness away. She made a swift decision. 'I'm going to the church to put flowers on my parents' graves. I won't be long. I could meet you in the coffee shop in half an hour, if you like?'

'Are you going to the church at Penhally?'

'Yes.' She frowned. 'Why?'

He sighed. 'That's where Susie and Kevin are buried. I ought to put some flowers on their grave. I know I should take Joey with me, but I haven't been able to face going to the churchyard yet, and I don't want him to see me all choked up.'

'The first time's the hardest,' Flora said. 'Why don't you

come with me? I'm putting flowers there myself—but, if you find you could do with talking to someone, I won't be far away.'

'Are you sure? I won't be in your way or anything?'

'Of course you won't. Look, I've just picked some daffodils from the garden. I'll split them with you.'

'Really?'

The relief in his tone decided her. 'Really. See you at the church in ten minutes.'

She drove to the church and parked on the gravelled car park outside the churchyard wall. It was such a quiet, peaceful spot, overlooking the bay; her parents had enjoyed sitting on the bench on the cliffs on Sunday afternoons.

Tom was waiting for her in the little lych gate, and her heart skipped a beat as he smiled at her. 'Thanks so much for this, Flora.'

'No worries.' She handed him half the flowers.

He stared at the daffodils and swallowed hard. 'Susie used to love spring flowers. The first thing she did when she and Kevin got the house was to plant spring bulbs. I remember she was so excited at having her own garden instead of just a window-box in her old flat in St Piran. I didn't get it at all because I was happy with my flat and not having to bother with weeding or mowing the lawn, but…' He grimaced. 'I guess I still can't believe she's gone.'

'I know what you mean. I find myself talking about my parents as if they're still here,' Flora said softly.

He rested his hand on her shoulder; even though she was wearing a sweater and a coat, it was as if she could feel the warmth of his skin against hers, and it sent a ripple of pure desire all the way down her spine.

'I really appreciate the way you've been here for me,' he said.

'Hey, that's what friends are for,' she said lightly, and turned away before she did something really stupid. Like standing on tiptoe, reaching up and brushing her mouth against his. 'Have you got something to put the flowers in?'

'No.' He looked horrified. 'It didn't even occur to me.'

'If Susie and Kevin are the first people you've lost, then of course you wouldn't think about it. It's something you find out the hard way.' She'd guessed he hadn't had a chance to think about the practicalities. 'Don't be too hard on yourself.' She produced a jam jar and a plastic bottle of water from her tote bag. 'The local florist sells cone-shaped vases that you just push into the ground for fresh flowers, but this will keep the flowers nice for now.'

'Flora, thank you.' He looked surprised and relieved in equal measure. 'I can't believe you thought of that, too.'

She shrugged off his praise and patted his shoulder. 'I'll come and find you when I've finished, shall I?'

She took the previous week's flowers from her parents' grave, tidied up the area, arranged the new daffodils, and then went to join Tom. His face was set and she could see that his eyelashes were damp. She remembered the first time she'd visited her parents' grave; she'd gone alone, and ended up bawling her eyes out on her knees in front of their grave, really wishing she'd had someone to hold her. Right now, Tom needed that same strength. And this was something she could do.

'Come here,' she said softly, and slid her arms round him, holding him close.

Tom closed his eyes, wrapped his arms round Flora, and rested his face against her hair. She smelled of roses and something else he couldn't quite pin down. And something of her warmth and strength seemed to flow into him as she held him, to the point where he was able to cope again.

'Sorry about that,' he said. 'I'm not usually that weak.'

Though, for the life of him, he couldn't let her go. He needed to feel her arms round him.

'It's not weak to admit you miss someone,' Flora said.

Wasn't it? He was a firefighter. He was meant to be in control. Someone who coped brilliantly in the worst kind of emergencies. Why was he going to pieces now, after putting flowers on his sister's grave? 'It feels it.'

'It's grief,' she reminded him gently. 'And it makes you feel all kinds of weird things. You might feel angry that the ones you love have left you, you might feel as if it's your fault and you're being punished for something, you might feel numb— and it's all OK. You get through it eventually.'

'It feels never-ending,' he admitted. 'Work's easy. I know what I'm doing there. But home… I never would've believed it's so hard to be a parent. How much worry there is.'

'It's not an easy job at all, especially when you're on your own,' Flora reassured him. 'And what you're feeling right now is perfectly normal. Give yourself a break, Tom.'

'Maybe.' He dropped a kiss on the top of her head. 'Do you mind if we get out of here?'

'Sure.' She paused. 'A walk on the beach might help.'

'The sea always makes me feel grounded,' he agreed. 'I loved coming to the bay when I was a child. It didn't matter if it was summer or the middle of winter—the wind would blow my worries away and the sound of the sea would silence all the doubts.' And with her by his side, it made him feel as if he *could* do things. As if he wasn't making a total mess of his life, outside work. Her warmth and her calmness soothed him even more than the sound of the sea.

They headed down the cliff path to the beach. The tide was half-out and the sea was calm, the waves rumbling onto the shore and swishing out again. They walked in silence for a while, and eventually Tom turned to Flora.

'I've been thinking—you and Joey. Are you really sure it's all right for you to have him for so long?'

'Of course it is.'

'I feel I'm taking advantage of you. And I need to sort out paying you.'

She shook her head. 'I don't want any money, Tom.'

'But you're looking after my nephew and you're giving him breakfast and dinner. I can't expect you to do it all just out of the goodness of your heart. That's not fair.'

'I don't mind,' Flora said. 'If anything, it's going to be nice to have a bit of company.' She still found the house a bit empty in the mornings, half expecting her dad to come in from seeing to the chickens or her mum to come in from the garden with some herbs or some flowers. Not that she could tell Tom that without sounding needy, and she didn't want him worrying that she wasn't stable enough to care for Joey properly.

'Then thank you.' He bit his lip. 'Poor Joey's finding it hard to adjust to change.'

'It must be hard for you, too.'

He nodded. 'And I can't even bring myself to go over to my sister's house and sort out her stuff, even though I know I should. I did a kind of grab raid when Joey was at school, the first week. I went there with a suitcase and got his clothes and his toys from his room. I've probably missed something important, something that really matters to him, and I know I shouldn't be so selfish—but I just can't handle it. I kept waiting for Susie to walk into the room and she just didn't, and it all felt so wrong…' He shook his head, grimacing. 'Sorry, I'm being really self-indulgent and you've had it harder than me, losing both your parents.'

She took his hand and squeezed it. 'It always hurts to lose someone you love. Look, I could come with you if you like, and help you sort through the stuff. It really helped me not to be on my own when I had to sort through my parents' things—Kate Tremayne from the surgery was really kind and helped me. It made a huge difference.'

'I might take you up on that.' His fingers tightened round hers. 'Thanks.'

'I've been thinking. Something else that might help Joey— you could try inviting one or two of his friends home for tea, when you're on a day off.'

'I don't think he has any friends,' Tom said. 'He did get a couple of invites, the first week back at school, but when I tried inviting the kids back the mums made excuses, and there haven't been any invites since.' He sighed. 'I don't know whether it's because he's so quiet and hardly talks, and they find that hard to deal with; or whether the other kids see Joey as being "different" because his parents died and they don't like him.'

She nodded. 'Other children can be cruel.'

Tom raised an eyebrow. 'That sounds personal.'

'Probably,' she admitted. 'My parents were elderly—Mum was forty-three when she had me, and Dad was ten years older than her. Everyone else's parents were around twenty years younger than them, so the kids at school always wanted to know if they were my grandparents, and refused to believe me when I said they were my parents. Then they used to say I was weird because my dad had grey hair.'

'That's horrible.' And that, Tom thought, was what was really at the root of her shyness. The way the children at school had made her feel like an outsider, rejecting her and mocking her; something like that would stick and make you worry about how other people saw you. And it would make you wary of others as you grew older. 'And you're not weird. Not at all.'

'It was just childish nonsense.' She shrugged. 'It doesn't bother me now.'

He wasn't so sure about that, but held his tongue. 'Did you lose your parents very long ago?' he asked.

'Last summer. Dad had a stroke. He was the love of Mum's life and she just gave up after he died—I know physiologically there's no such thing as a broken heart, but I honestly think that's why she died. Without Dad, she couldn't carry on. I buried her the month after.' She dragged in a breath. 'I hate just having a little wooden cross and a plastic pot I stick in the ground for flowers, but the stonemason says he can't put the headstone on for another couple of months.'

'So you understand exactly how Joey's feeling right now.' Guilt flooded through Tom. 'I'm sorry, I didn't mean to rub salt in your wounds.'

'You're not. And you,' she said softly, 'I know how you're feeling now, too. What you said about your sister's house—it was like that for me at the farmhouse. I guess I could've sold up, but I didn't want to—it's my home. So in the end I painted the walls a different colour and moved the furniture around and changed the colours of the cushions, just to get it into my head that things were different now and Mum and Dad aren't coming back.' She paused. 'It's going to take a while until you get used to it, Tom, so be kind to yourself.'

He was still holding her hand and he rubbed the pad of his thumb over the back of her hand. 'Can I buy you lunch? As a friend,' he added swiftly.

Not that he needed to say that, Flora thought. It was pretty obvious Tom wasn't going to be interested in her as anything other than a friend; she was way too mousy and boring. 'That'd be nice,' she said.

'If I follow you back to your place, we can drop your car off and I'll drive us,' Tom suggested.

They ended up at the Smugglers' Rest, just up the coast; and over a leisurely lunch they discovered that they had a lot in common. They both enjoyed the same kind of music and both were fans of historical crime novels—though Flora found out that Tom preferred action movies and hated the romantic comedies she enjoyed. And she couldn't remember the last time she'd enjoyed someone's company so much. When he'd opened up to her in the churchyard, it had made her feel close to him—to the point where she'd actually stopped feeling shy with him. They'd gone past that. She felt as comfortable with Tom now as she did with the people she worked with; and the fact that he seemed to listen to what she said, was interested in her views, made her feel more confident than she'd felt outside work since…since for ever, she thought.

Eventually, Tom glanced at his watch and gave a start. 'I've got to pick Joey up from school in a quarter of an hour! I can't believe how fast time's gone. I've really enjoyed having lunch with you, Flora.'

'Me, too,' she said, meaning it.

He tipped his head slightly on one side. 'Come with me to meet Joey?'

Flora pushed away the tempting thought that Tom might want her company for a bit longer. He was simply being practical; if he dropped her home first, he'd be late for school. 'OK.'

Joey was the last one out of the classroom and, although several of the children were lingering in the playground while their mums chatted, nobody made a move to speak to him. Flora's heart went out to him; poor little mite, he was having such a tough time.

Joey was silent on the way to the car, but when Tom strapped him in he asked, 'Are we going to see Banjo?'

'I do need to drop Flora back at the farm before we go home—but, if Flora doesn't mind, we can stay for a few minutes.'

Joey's faint smile said it all for him.

Tom stayed long enough to have a cup of tea with Flora,

and Joey accepted a glass of milk and a cookie; but then Tom called his nephew over from playing with the dog. 'We need to let Flora get on, and I have to cook you something for tea. We need to go, sweetheart.'

Joey nodded, but said nothing.

Tom's eyes were sad as he glanced at his nephew, and Flora's heart contracted. If only she could wave a magic wand for them. But they were going to have to muddle through this together and learn to bond and talk to each other and trust each other.

'We'll see you on Wednesday morning, then, Flora,' Tom said, and, to her surprise, kissed her on the cheek.

She felt the betraying wash of colour flood into her cheeks. Obviously Tom was a fairly tactile person; the kiss didn't mean anything at all, and this was just friendship. Yet she could feel the touch of his lips against her skin all evening, and it sent a mixture of warmth and excitement bubbling through her.

Tuesday was busy, thanks to a cold snap. Flora was on duty at the surgery all day on the minor injuries clinic, and there was a steady stream of people coming in to see her after falling over, most of them with hands that hurt. Several of them had very obvious signs of Colles' fractures. 'I'm going to have to send you to St Piran's for an X-ray and backslab,' she explained to the first of her patients. 'Everyone puts their hands out to save themselves when they fall, and if you land awkwardly you can end up breaking your wrist. You'll be in a cast for a couple of weeks until it heals. The good news is that casts are lightweight nowadays, so it won't get too much in the way, but the bad news is that you're going to have to get someone else to do all your lifting and carrying until your arm's healed.'

It felt odd not to see Tom and Joey in the evening. Flora was cross with herself for getting too involved, too fast. For pity's sake, she knew that Tom had other demands on his time. His job was incredibly difficult, and he had to get used to being a stand-in dad to his nephew. He wasn't going to have time to keep coming over to the farm and seeing her. And, unless she was looking after Joey, he didn't really even have a reason for coming to see her. 'I'm being ridiculous about this,' she told her dog. 'Worse than a teenager with a crush—and I haven't got a crush on Tom Nicholson.'

Banjo regarded her steadily, as if he didn't believe her.

She sighed. 'All right, so I think he's gorgeous. And it's not just the way he looks. He's a nice guy and there's something about him that makes me feel more...well, confident. He listens to me, so I don't feel like a bumbling idiot when I'm with him. I like the way his mind works, I like the way he puts other people first, and I like the way he's trying so hard to fit his life round Joey, rather than making Joey fit round him.' She bit her lip. 'But I've got to be practical about this, because he's way out of my league.'

But all the same she was pleased the next morning to hear the crunch of the gravel as Tom parked outside.

'Have you had breakfast yet?' she asked as she met Tom and Joey at the door.

He shook his head. 'I'll get something at the station.'

'It's as easy to make breakfast for three as it is for two.'

'Thanks, but I need to get going or I'll be late for work.'

Of course. And she was being ridiculous, feeling disappointed that he wasn't staying. At her age, she should know better. 'See you tonight, then.' She smiled at him. 'Have a nice day.'

'You, too. Bye, Joey.' Tom ruffled his nephew's hair awkwardly, and Joey gave him a pained look. Tom was clearly careful not to react in front of the boy, but Flora saw his shoulders slump as he headed back to his car. Every time Joey rejected him, she had a feeling that it cracked Tom's heart that little bit more.

'So what would you like for breakfast, Joey? I was thinking about French toast. Have you ever had French toast?'

The little boy shook his head.

'Do you fancy playing chef?'

His face lit up and he went to fetch a tea-towel from the drawer. Flora couldn't help smiling as he tucked it round himself to keep his school uniform clean. 'Good boy—well remembered.'

Joey seemed to thoroughly enjoy helping her beat the egg with vanilla essence and dip the bread into it. While the French toast was cooking, she sliced up some fruit onto two plates, then put the cooked French toast next to it.

'Nice?' she asked after Joey had taken a bite.

He nodded.

'Score out of five?'

He thought about it, then held up his right palm with all four fingers and thumb outstretched.

'Five? Excellent.' She beamed at him. 'We make a good team, Joey Barber.'

She washed up the breakfast things, then took him to school. 'Now, Joey, I know you don't like holding people's hands very much, but there's a fair bit of traffic here and I need to know you're safe, so I need you to hold my hand from the car to the playground, OK?'

He nodded and let her hold his hand.

For one crazy moment, Flora thought, This is what it would be like to take my own child to school. Then she shook herself. How silly. She didn't even date, so marriage and children were hardly an option.

But, oh, how she missed being part of a family. How she'd love a family of her own, somewhere she'd be accepted for herself. She adored Banjo, but the dog could only listen to her, not talk back, and she wasn't quite soppy enough to believe that the dog understood every word she said to her. Right now, she was rattling around on her own in the farmhouse. Lonely. As an only child, she didn't even have nieces and nephews to spoil—not now, and not in the future. So, unless she could do something to overcome her shyness and start dating, it was pretty unlikely that she'd ever have a family of her own again.

Though where did you meet people? At work wasn't an option for her; apart from the fact that the male doctors in the practice were already married, most of her patients were children. Even if she did end up treating an adult male who happened to be single, there was no way she'd be unprofessional enough to ask him out on a date.

And she wasn't one for parties or going clubbing. Which left a dating agency—and no way would she be able to meet up with a complete stranger. She'd spend the whole evening beetroot red, fumbling for words and feeling too awkward and embarrassed to relax, wishing herself back safely at home. It wouldn't be like the other day, when she'd sat in the Smugglers', chatting to Tom. Or like this morning, when she and Joey had made French toast.

She glanced at the little boy. Joey stood apart from the other children in the playground; he'd always been one of the quiet ones, but he was really cutting himself off. Was he scared that if he let someone close, he'd lose them, the way he'd lost his parents? That would explain why he was refusing to let Tom hug him or ride on his shoulders, the way Tom had said he'd done while Susie and Kevin had still been alive.

Maybe playing with Banjo would help. Bonding with the dog might help him bond with his uncle again, and gradually he'd learn to open up to other people.

The doors opened and the classroom assistant stood there to welcome the children in. 'See you at five, sweetheart,' Flora said, and watched him walk in through the doors before she headed off to work.

She texted Tom to let him know that Joey was safely at school, and got a brief text back saying just '*Thanks*'. Well, he was at work, and he was busy. She'd been an idiot to hope that he'd send a personal message back. That kiss on her cheek the other night had been completely platonic, and she was acting like a teenager. She put it firmly out of her mind, got on with her work, and then met Joey from after-school club at five.

'How was your day?' she asked.

He shrugged and said nothing.

OK. She'd try something less emotional and see if he responded to that. 'Do you like drawing?'

He nodded, to her relief.

'Great. You can draw some pictures when we get back, if you like.' She'd popped to the shops at lunchtime and bought a sketchpad and pencils; she'd also picked up some more books from the library. Joey drew pictures and played with Banjo while she prepared dinner; then she read him some stories while the veg steamed and the shepherd's pie cooked. Over dinner, he told her shyly that a policeman had come in for show-and-tell and he was the daddy of Mitchell in his class, and Flora had a lightbulb moment: this was something that might help Tom and Joey bond.

Finally, at a quarter past seven, Tom rang the doorbell.

He tried to make a fuss of Joey, but the little boy was having none of it; he turned away and concentrated on turning the pages of his book.

Seeing the hurt in Tom's face at the rejection, Flora switched on the kettle. 'How was your day?' she asked.

'Pretty eventful. I had to break into a house to rescue a family,' he said.

'Was it a fire?'

'No—it was carbon monoxide poisoning.'

'What happened?' She put a mug of coffee in front of him.

'The husband thought he had a bug or something. He felt a bit dizzy and sleepy, but he didn't have a temperature so he went in to work. He felt a bit better during the day, so he rang home—he knew his wife had been feeling a bit rough, too, and had stayed at home with the youngest because she had a vomiting bug, but then his wife didn't answer the phone or her mobile. He was worried in case she'd had to take the little one to hospital or something, so he rang their neighbour and asked him to take a look. He could see her car outside, but there was no answer when he knocked on the door. He looked through the window and saw her collapsed on the floor, so he called the emergency services.'

Flora winced. 'Lucky for them that the neighbour was there.'

'We broke in and got them out; then the ambulance arrived and the paramedics put them on oxygen.'

'Was that enough, or did they have to go to hospital?'

Tom couldn't remember talking about his job to a girlfriend before; it felt odd, chatting to someone who understood where he was coming from, but he rather liked it. 'The oxygen was enough,' he said. 'The paramedics put them on an ECG monitor and the trace was OK, so they're going to be fine. We took a look in the house and could see that the flames in the gas fire in the living room were yellow, not blue.'

'Which I take it is a problem?'

'Very much so,' Tom said. 'They called in a gas engineer to sort it out, and it turned out there was a blocked flue as well as the dodgy gas fire. It's all sorted now, and he rang us to thank us for saving his wife and youngest child's life, and to let us know what had happened.' He smiled. 'I like days like today, where I can actually fix things and make them right. How about you?'

'I was doing routine vaccinations today—back at the nursery, finishing off the ones I didn't do on Friday—and I was at the surgery this afternoon. Joey and I have had a nice evening together. We read some stories.'

Tom took the hint. 'Which was your favourite, Joey?' he asked, hoping that this time his nephew would respond.

'The one about the dog,' Joey said.

'We're going to choose the next ones together, so I don't pick ones he's already read,' Flora explained.

'I drawed Flora a picture. Me and Banjo,' Joey said.

'It's on the fridge.' Flora removed the magnet and handed the picture to Tom.

Tom suppressed the wish that his nephew had drawn him a picture, too. Flora was doing so much for him; it was churlish and ridiculous to be envious of her. Yet she seemed to be able to get through to the little boy where he couldn't, and he really wished he knew her secret.

'Can I get you something to eat?' Flora asked.

'No, you're fine. Thanks for offering, but I get a meal at work before the end of my shift.' He could see that she was taking it as a personal rejection and smiled to soften it. 'But this coffee is fabulous. Just what I need.'

There was another awkward silence while Tom wondered what he should say next to his nephew.

Flora, as if sensing his dilemma, stepped in. 'Joey had show-and-tell in class today,' she said.

'What did you see, Jojo?' Tom asked, picking up her obvious cue.

'A policeman.'

'Did you try on his hat?'

'And his handcuffs,' Joey said solemnly.

So Joey had enjoyed that, Tom thought. Would he, perhaps, like a firefighter to go in for show and tell? His gaze met Flora's, and she nodded very slightly, as if guessing what was in his mind. 'Have you ever had a firefighter in for show-and-tell?' he asked.

Joey shook his head.

'I'll have to check the schedule with my boss, but if you want me to I can maybe arrange to bring the engine and the crew out and show your class around. Obviously, provided we don't have to go off to put out a fire.'

Joey's eyes went wide.

'Would you like that, Joey?' Flora asked softly.

Joey nodded, and Tom felt the muscles of his shoulders relax. 'I'll have a chat with my boss and your teacher, then.' And maybe this would help Joey bond with him again. It would be something he could talk to his classmates about, maybe.

Tom meant to kiss Flora on the cheek again when he took Joey home, but somehow he ended up brushing his mouth against hers instead. Her mouth was soft and sweet and she tasted of vanilla. He had to resist the temptation to kiss her again; her eyes had gone wide and the amber flecks were even more obvious, and she looked utterly adorable.

And he really shouldn't be doing this.

'Flora, I—'

'It's OK.' She shook her head, clearly not wanting to discuss it. 'You'd better get Joey to bed. See you in the morning. 'Night, Joey!'

The little boy waved, and Tom mentally called himself all kinds of a fool. Flora was a lifesaver for him, right now, and he'd better not do anything to jeopardise it.

CHAPTER SIX

THE next morning, Tom looked wary when he dropped Joey off. Flora strove to be cheerful and polite and breezy so he wouldn't think she was still thrown by that kiss—even though she was, and her lips were still tingling at the memory of his mouth against hers. She knew how pathetic it was, having a crush on the most gorgeous firefighter in the crew. Of course he wouldn't be interested in boring, mousy her. They were just *friends*.

'Joey, do you like porridge, like the Three Bears had?' she asked.

He nodded.

'You can help me chop the fruit to put on top,' she said, 'and then we'll have a story while the porridge is cooking. I found a really good one where the bears get their revenge on Goldilocks; would you like to hear that one?'

He nodded again.

'Say bye-bye to Uncle Tom,' she said with a smile.

'Bye-bye.' Joey gave a tiny wave.

'See you later, Tom. Have a nice day,' she said brightly.

That was definitely a fake smile, Tom thought as he drove to work. Flora was clearly wary of him—and no wonder. He'd really messed up last night. Fancy kissing her like that. Why on earth hadn't he controlled himself? But he found her irresistible. And he hadn't been able to stop thinking about her ever since that hug outside the church.

When he'd kissed her on the cheek it had been spontaneous. Friendly. But last night's kiss—though equally chaste—had thrown him. He'd even dreamed about Flora last night. Dreams that set his pulse racing and made his body surge when he thought about it.

But she clearly didn't think the same way. So he needed to keep himself strictly under control in future.

Tonight, he'd bring flowers when he picked Joey up. He'd apologise, tell her that she had nothing to worry about—and he'd keep it platonic in future.

Thursday morning was Flora's clinic at the high school, where anyone could drop in and talk to her privately if they had any worries. She was also doing the second of the three-stage HPV vaccinations of the Year Eight girls. She could hear them chattering in the queue; one of them was talking about how her boyfriend had kissed her for the first time, and Flora thought of the way Tom had kissed her last night and how it had sent heat all the way through her body.

Oh, how juvenile. She really, *really* had to get a grip. She was twenty-four, not fourteen.

She'd just finished vaccinating one class when the school receptionist came hurrying through. 'Flora, there's been an accident. The fire brigade are on their way, but two of the Year Eight lads decided to skip lessons and go skating on the pond—they went straight through. Luckily one of the sixth formers decided to go to the library halfway through private study and heard them yelling for help; she had the sense to call the emergency services on her mobile phone and then came to tell me.'

The pond had had a reputation as a skating rink in Flora's days at the school; and, no matter how often the children were warned not to do it, there was always at least one every year willing to take the risk. As the boys had fallen through the ice and must have been there for a while, they were severely at risk of developing immersion hypothermia; they might even need hospital treatment. 'OK, I'm on my way. There are space blankets in the PE department, aren't there?' At the receptionist's nod, she said, 'Can you get someone to bring some through—and some spare clothing and towels, please?' As soon as the boys were out of the pond, the first thing she needed to do was to get them into dry clothes and start warming them up, heads and torsos first.

'I'll ring through now,' the receptionist said.

Flora took her medical bag and hurried over to the pond, pulling her coat on as she went. It was barely above freezing; why on earth had the boys been so daft? She could see the fire engine there; the crew had ladders out and one fireman was crawling along it towards the boys so he could pull them out. Her heart missed a beat. Even though she couldn't see the fireman's face and she knew that several of the fire crew were just as tall and brawny as Tom, she knew instinctively that it was him.

Please, let him be safe.

Rob Werrick, one of the PE teachers, came out with a space blanket, spare tracksuit bottoms and sweatshirts, and towels. 'It's Danny and Harry from Year Eight,' he said as he glanced at the pond. 'When I heard what had happened, I should've guessed those two would be involved.' He rolled his eyes. 'What on earth did they think they were doing?'

'In my day, there were stories about people skating on the pond. They probably thought it sounded like fun,' Flora suggested.

'Taking a huge risk, more like.' Rob sighed. 'They've all been warned to stay away from the pond. But do they ever listen?'

'Teenage boys,' Flora said ruefully. 'I think they have se-
lective hearing.'

She could hear Tom talking to the boys, explaining how
he was going to get them out and what they needed to do. He
brought the first one back with him across the ladder, and kept
the other one talking as he did so—no doubt, Flora thought, so
he could keep a check on the boy's level of consciousness.

'Hi, Flora.' He smiled at her. 'Well, young Danny, I'm
handing you over to safe hands now to get you checked over
while I go and fish your mate out of the pond.' He winked at
Flora, then headed back to the ladder.

'Come on, Danny, let's get you inside and get you out of
those wet clothes and warmed up.' She hurried him into the
nearest building.

'I can't get undressed in front of you. You're a girl,' Danny
mumbled.

Usually Year Eight boys managed to make her blush or
stutter; most of them were as tall as she was and it took her
right back to her schooldays, when she'd been awkward and
painfully shy and just hadn't fitted in. But Tom's words had
bolstered her confidence: he'd treated Danny as a child and
made it clear he was handing the boy over to someone whose
opinion he respected. To *her*.

'You're a child,' Flora said crisply, 'and I'm a nurse. I'm
not interested in your naked body. You're wet and very, very
cold, and I need you to get into dry clothes before I can assess
your breathing and your heart, OK?'

Danny muttered something she couldn't quite catch and
didn't look her in the eye.

She rolled her eyes. 'If it makes you feel better, I'll turn
my back. Dry off and get dressed, please—and don't rub your
skin, pat it.'

Tom came in, a few moments later. 'What are we going to
do with Harry?'

'Same as Danny. Wet clothes off, blot your skin with a towel—don't rub,' she warned, 'and then dry clothes on and a space blanket round you.'

Harry looked as embarrassed as Danny. 'I can't—'

'I've already had that conversation with Danny. I'm turning my back,' Flora said.

She could see the amusement in Tom's eyes but, to his credit, he didn't laugh.

Once the boys were dressed in dry clothes and had space blankets round them, she blotted their hair dry and then put woolly hats on them.

'Why do we have to wear hats indoors?' Harry asked, his teeth chattering.

'Because you lose the most heat from your head—the hat stops you losing the heat,' Flora explained. 'And you're both shivering, which is a good sign.' It showed that their bodies were trying to bring their temperature up again rather than just giving up.

'Is there anything else you need?' Rob Werrick asked.

'A mug of hot chocolate each would be good—not boiling hot, but warm so it helps to get their temperature back up,' Flora said.

'I'll make you both a coffee at the same time. Milk, sugar?'

'I'm fine,' Flora said.

'Just milk for me, please,' Tom said.

After the warm drink, Danny and Harry finally stopped shivering. Flora took their pulse and blood pressure, and listened to their hearts. 'You're going to be fine,' she told them. 'You were incredibly lucky this time, but for pity's sake *never* do anything like this again. It really isn't worth the risk. And nobody's going to think you're cool or clever if you end up in hospital.'

'Ice needs to be at least twelve centimetres thick to bear

your weight,' Tom said, 'and this wasn't anywhere near thick enough.'

'It looked thick enough,' Danny said, looking mutinous.

'But it wasn't. You went straight through it.'

'Dad said he skated on the pond when he was here,' Harry said.

'Your dad might have been teasing you.'

'No, he really did it.'

'Then he took a very big risk. The pond's too deep for you to haul yourself out onto the ice once you've gone through it. And you two are very lucky that someone heard you yelling for help. If you'd been stuck in that water for thirty minutes, you might not have survived,' Tom said grimly. 'Your body temperature would've dropped so low that you could've died—and think of how your families would've felt, losing you.'

Danny and Harry looked at each other, but said nothing.

'Are our parents going to have to know about this?' Danny asked eventually.

'Of course they are,' Flora said. 'Your parents need to know what happened. I'll be the one speaking to your mums and reassuring them that you're both OK and you haven't got hypothermia.'

'Mum's *so* going to ground me,' Harry said. 'And she's going to ban my games console for a month.'

'Me, too,' Danny said. 'It's not fair.'

'And it was fair of you both to skip lessons, go onto the ice to show off to your mates, and end up risking the lives of the fire crew?' Flora asked.

Harry's cheeks reddened. 'I s'pose not.'

'Danny?' she prompted.

He pulled a face. 'No.'

'Is there something you both want to say to Mr Nicholson

here, then?' Flora asked. Both boys hung their heads. 'Sorry,' they mumbled, their faces bright red with embarrassment.

'And?' she prompted.

Danny looked at her. 'What?'

'He saved your life,' she pointed out quietly. 'Which I think might be worth two little words your parents probably made you say when you were little—and you've clearly forgotten.'

They both went even redder and muttered, 'Thank you.'

'Right. Better get back to your lessons.' Flora folded her arms. 'And you might find life an awful lot easier if you stop to think things through before you act next time, OK?'

The boys nodded, looking ashamed, and shuffled out of the room.

'So you have a stern side, Flora Loveday,' Tom said, sounding amused.

'When people do really stupid things and put others at risk, then yes.' She shrugged. 'You don't need to shout or swear to get your point across.'

'No, somehow I don't think they're going to forget what you said to them.' He sighed. 'I wanted to shake the pair of them, I admit. It was a really stupid thing to do. Ice can vary in thickness across a pond—one part can be safe, but put one foot on a weak area, and you'll go straight through into the water.' He grimaced. 'It isn't the first time I've rescued someone from falling through ice, and it won't be the last.'

Flora looked at him. 'They're fine, but are you OK? You had to crawl out on the ice.'

'On a ladder. I'm fine. I'm wearing a drysuit and several layers underneath—and Rob got me that coffee, so that's warmed me up.' His eyes crinkled at the corners as he looked at her. 'I'd better get back to work. See you later.'

'See you,' she said, smiling back.

* * *

After school, Joey spent the afternoon racing round with Banjo, and he was asleep when Tom arrived to pick him up. Banjo stood next to Joey, on guard duty, and Tom ruffled the dog's fur. 'You're a good boy,' he said softly. Then he turned to Flora and handed her the flowers.

'They're lovely, Tom, but you really don't need to bring me flowers.'

'I do, today.'

She looked puzzled. 'Why?'

'Last night.' He took a deep breath. 'About that…I owe you an apology. I didn't mean to come on so strong.'

She didn't meet his eyes. 'It's not a problem. I know you didn't mean it that way.'

Something in her voice alerted Tom: Flora obviously thought she wasn't attractive enough for any man to want to kiss her. How on earth had she got that idea? He cupped her face in one hand and gently moved her chin so she was looking him straight in the eye. 'Flora, you do know you're beautiful, don't you?'

'Me? *Beautiful*?' Her face was filled with astonishment. 'You must be joking. I'm nothing like a WAG.'

Was that her definition of beauty? It wasn't his. 'I'm glad you're not. You're not caked in make-up, and you don't spend hours doing your nails and dyeing your hair. Yours is a natural beauty. And very, very real.'

She went bright pink.

'And then you have depths. You're not one of these shallow, boring women. You're kind and you're sweet and…' And he wanted her very, very badly. Too much to be able to resist. 'Flora.' He breathed her name, dipped his head and kissed her again. This time with intent. His mouth moved over hers, teasing and coaxing, until she gave a tiny sigh, slid her free arm round his neck and kissed him back.

'I'm not going to apologise for that one,' he said when he broke the kiss. 'Just so you know, I meant it.'

She blushed again and her lips parted, as if inviting him to kiss her some more.

'You taste of vanilla,' he said softly.

'It's lip salve.'

He smiled. 'Keep wearing it. I like it.'

She flushed again. 'Tom, you can't— I mean, I'm not your type.'

'No? So what do you think is my type?'

'Someone glamorous. Someone tall.' She swallowed hard. 'Someone *thin*.'

He'd begun to be bored with glamour. Height didn't matter. And he loathed dating women who nibbled on a stick of celery and refused pudding in case it made them put on a few grams; he much preferred the company of women who actually enjoyed eating out with him.

'Wrong on all counts,' he told her softly. 'And why are you putting yourself down? You have delicious curves, Flora. Curves that make me want to...' He slid both hands down her sides, moulding her curves. 'You're lovely. Luscious.'

He took the flowers from her hand, put them on the table, then scooped her up and sat down on the sofa, pulling her onto his lap. 'I know I probably shouldn't be doing this. I don't have the right to ask to start seeing you—my life is complicated, and I'm already taking way too much advantage of your good nature.' He stole a kiss. 'But I've been thinking about you all day. All week, really,' he admitted ruefully. 'I haven't been able to get you out of my head since the day I met you.'

She shook her head. 'But that's not possible.'

'Why's it so hard to believe? Flora, you're a pocket Venus. You have the most gorgeous mouth. And you taste...' he brushed his mouth against hers again '...like heaven.'

* * *

Self-consciousness washed through her. He'd just called her a pocket Venus. She knew she was just frumpy and overweight. And right now she was probably crushing his legs, and he was doing the macho firefighter thing and pretending she wasn't.

'Flora.' He kissed the tip of her nose. 'You look worried. Do you want me to back off?'

'No-o.'

'You don't sound very sure.' He twined the end of her ponytail round his finger. 'OK, let me ask you a different question. Will you go out with me?'

'I...' Heat flooded into her face. 'Look, I, um, haven't dated much.' And she certainly hadn't ever had a serious boyfriend. 'I'm not very good at this.' She bit her lip. 'And you're...'

'I'm what?' he prompted gently.

Sex on legs. Not that anything would drag that admission from her. 'You must have women falling at your feet all the time,' she said unhappily. Gorgeous women. Glamorous women who were used to dating and had all the right social skills.

'I admit, I get teased at work for having a fan club. There are a few women who insist on baking me cakes.'

She'd just bet there were.

'And some of them are in their eighties,' Tom said.

Maybe, but she was pretty sure that a good deal more of them would be around her own age.

'Some of them think of me as a surrogate grandson who rescues their cat and checks that their smoke alarms are working properly. I'm polite to everyone who makes me cakes, I thank them for their kindness but I don't make a habit of going around kissing women.'

Which wasn't the same thing as saying that they didn't kiss him.

He kissed her again. 'I guess I'm trying to say that there's

something about you. I can't get you out of my head. And
I really, really like kissing you.' He caught her bottom lip
between his, just to prove it.

And this time she couldn't help kissing him back.

When he broke the kiss, he settled her against him, wrapping his arms round her. 'You know, this is the first time
my world's felt right this year,' he said softly. 'So can I see
you?'

'Tom.' She stroked his face. 'I wasn't expecting this to
happen.'

'Do you mind?'

'It scares me a bit,' she admitted. 'I'm not used to this.'

'I'm not going to hurt you, Flora. I like you. A lot.'

'Are you sure this isn't—well, just gratitude?'

'Because you're helping me with Joey? Given that I was
dreaming about you last night,' Tom said, 'and you'd really
be blushing if I told you exactly what was happening in that
dream…No. It's definitely not just gratitude.'

She blushed anyway. Tom had been having raunchy dreams
about her?

'You're adorable,' he said softly. 'Actually, I love it when
you go all pink and flustered. It makes me want to kiss you
and fluster you some more. And your eyes are amazing. They
have these little amber flecks in them. Like gold.'

That was what people always said when they knew you
weren't drop-dead gorgeous and they tried to compliment
you: they said you had nice eyes.

'And your ears.'

Now, that she hadn't expected. She stared at him in surprise. 'My ears?'

'Uh-huh.' He nibbled one lobe, very gently, then kissed his
way down the sensitive spots at the side of her neck, making
her shiver. 'And your mouth. It's a perfect rosebud. It's beautiful. Tempting. Irresistible.' He kissed her again, to make the

point. 'And your curves are delicious.' He kept his arms very firmly round her. 'I like you, Flora. Very much. As a person, because you're warm and sweet and kind and you make the world seem a better place.' He paused, making eye contact. 'And as a woman. I really, *really* like you as a woman.'

'I like you, too,' she admitted shyly. 'As a— As a man.'

'So how about we see where this takes us?'

She took a deep breath. 'OK. But, as far as Joey's concerned, you and I are just friends—which keeps things stable in his world and he isn't going to worry that suddenly neither of us will have time for him.'

'That's another thing,' Tom said softly. 'You think about other people. How things affect them. You're incredibly empathetic.'

'It's my job. I'm a nurse.'

'No, Flora, it's who you are,' he corrected. 'And it's yet another thing that draws me to you.'

She still found it hard to believe that Tom was serious—how could he possibly want her, when he could have his pick of the most gorgeous women in this part of Cornwall?—and yet his dark eyes were sincere. He wasn't spinning her a line.

Joey stirred and she wriggled off Tom's lap. 'Joey,' she said softly.

Tom stole a last kiss, then went to scoop his nephew off the beanbag. 'Come on, sweetheart. You're sleepy. Let's get you home.'

To Flora's surprise and pleasure, Joey didn't wriggle out of his arms and actually let Tom carry him to the car.

'See you tomorrow, Flora,' he said softly. 'And thank you.'

Flora still couldn't quite believe what had just happened: that Tom had actually sat with her on his lap, had kissed her and told her he thought she was gorgeous.

She pinched herself. It hurt. So she wasn't dreaming, then.

And the flowers he'd brought her were still on the table. She hadn't even put them in water yet; she'd been too caught up in the way Tom had cradled her on his lap and kissed her. She smiled and put the flowers in a vase—and she was still smiling when she fell asleep that night.

On Friday evening, Tom had news. 'I'm going to do the show-and-tell at Joey's class next week.'

'That's great—he'll enjoy that.'

'And there's something else—I play football in the local emergency services league. Our team's having a "dads and sons" match on Sunday morning, when I'm off duty. I'm going to take Joey; will you come with us?'

'I've never been to a football match.'

'Because you hate football?'

She wrinkled her nose. 'Well, it's not really my sort of thing.' And she'd been utterly hopeless at sport at school—always the last to be picked for any team.

'Ah, but this is different. And Joey and I could do with someone standing on the sidelines cheering for us,' Tom said.

Put like that, how could she refuse?

Then she thought of something. 'So you're working tomorrow?' Being Saturday, Joey wouldn't have school.

'Yes.'

'Do you want to bring Joey over?'

'I can't impose on you like that.' Before she could protest that it was fine and she didn't mind, he added softly, 'Kevin's parents are coming down to see him for the day. Actually, they're coming this evening and staying overnight, so I'd better get back and sort my place out, because it's a tip.' He smiled at her. 'The match on Sunday starts at ten so we'll pick you up at half past nine, OK?'

'Half-nine it is,' she agreed.

He kissed her swiftly but very, very sweetly. 'Sorry I have to go so soon—I would rather stay with you, but Joey needs to see his grandparents.'

'Of course he does. I understand, Tom.'

'I can't believe how lucky I am to have found you.' He stole a last kiss. 'We'll see you on Sunday morning.'

CHAPTER SEVEN

ON SUNDAY, Tom picked Flora up at half past nine on the dot and drove her to the playing field. She felt ridiculously shy as she climbed out of his car. Tom seemed to know everyone; people were coming up all the time to talk to him or clap him on the back and ask how many goals he thought he'd score in the match. And she didn't know a single one of them. Nobody from Penhally was here; this was a completely different crowd to what she'd been expecting. The only person she could see that she recognised was Megan Phillips—and Megan was standing on the sidelines, shoulders hunched and hands in her pockets, her body language making it very clear that she didn't want to talk to anyone.

This was awful. Just like one or two of her mums had confided to her about the baby and toddler group, the first time they'd been—everyone else knew each other and had bonded into a little group, and they weren't part of it. Flora wasn't part of this group, either.

Her advice to her mums had been to take a deep breath and start talking to someone, and they'd soon find something in common.

What a hypocrite she was—she couldn't even follow her own advice. She didn't have a clue what to say. What did she have in common with these glamorous women in their tight jeans, fashionable boots and waxed jackets? She couldn't even go over and talk to them about children, because Joey wasn't really hers. Besides, she only recognised a couple of the children on the pitch from Penhally, and a swift scan of the sidelines told her that their mums weren't at the match—they were obviously at home looking after the younger children.

In the end, she simply stood on the sidelines, watching Tom and Joey, thinking miserably that she was never going to fit in with Tom's crowd. Maybe they ought to stop this disaster of a relationship before it had really begun.

Megan shoved her hands deeper into her pockets. What an idiot she was, turning up to the father-and-son football match. And all to catch a glimpse of Josh. Stupid, really. Josh was only there because one of the emergency department doctors had got flu and had had to drop out. He didn't even have a child with him.

Though if things had been different, he would've done. A seven-year-old boy. A boy with Josh's indigo-blue eyes and ready smile, perhaps. A boy who adored his father and had grown up knowing how much he was loved by both his parents...

The back of her throat felt tight. There was no point in wishing things were different, because they weren't. She'd lost the baby. And more. She never would have a child of her own. The nearest she could get to it was through her work, saving the lives of other people's precious babies.

And that had to be enough.

She swallowed hard. She really shouldn't have come today. Better to leave now—before Josh saw her and started asking questions.

To her surprise, Flora discovered that she enjoyed watching the game and cheering as Tom scored a goal. She had a flask of hot chocolate in her basket ready for half-time, and had also spent the Saturday afternoon making a batch of brownies and cookies. She poured a small mug of hot chocolate for Joey; Tom simply stole her mug, deliberately sipped from exactly the same spot that she had, and gave her a smile that made her knees go weak. And suddenly it didn't matter that she was on her own on the sidelines; Tom and Joey wanted her there, and that was the main thing.

'Enjoying it?' Tom asked.

She smiled. 'Yes.' It wasn't a complete fib; now he and Joey were here with her, she was definitely enjoying it.

Josh spotted Megan on the sidelines. On her own. But why would she come to a football match? Unless...

'Pay attention, Josh! That was an easy pass. You should've scored.'

'Sorry, mate.' Josh held his hands up in acknowledgement of the fault. But all the same he couldn't help looking for Megan during the match, trying to catch her eye. When the whistle blew for half-time, he caught one of the others. 'Can you substitute me for a bit? Something I really need to do.'

'What, *now*?'

'Yes, now,' Josh said, clapping his team-mate's shoulder. If Megan was here, unless she was here as the medical support—which he very much doubted—it was to see him. And he couldn't pass up the chance that she might be ready to talk to him. To start sorting things out between them.

Except, when he reached the place he'd seen her, she wasn't there. He scanned the sidelines and couldn't see her there, either. Maybe she was in the car park.

But a swift search of the car park told him that Megan had gone.

Needing a moment to himself, he leaned against the bonnet of his own car. Why had she come here in the first place? He didn't have a clue what was going on in her head. But one thing he did know: they needed to talk. Properly.

Five minutes into the second half, one of the players fell to the ground and rolled onto his back, clutching his leg. The referee stopped the match. Automatically, Flora went over; her skills were needed, and that was enough to push her shyness and feelings of awkwardness into the background. 'I'm a nurse,' she explained. 'Can I do anything to help?'

The referee gave her a grateful look. 'Yes, please. This is Ian.'

'What happened, Ian?' she asked.

'My ankle's killing me,' he groaned.

'Can I take a look?'

He nodded, his face white with pain.

'I'll need to take your boot off. Is that OK?' When he gave his consent, she crouched down, removed his football boot and drew the sock down so she could see his ankle properly, then probed his ankle gently.

'Ow. That hurts,' Ian said.

'It's a pretty nasty sprain,' Flora said. 'Looks like you've landed awkwardly—you've twisted the joint and it's damaged your ligaments. I'm afraid you're not going to be able to play for the rest of the match. Did you hear a "pop" in your ankle when it happened?'

'Yes—and then it started hurting like crazy.'

'I'm pretty sure it's not a fracture, just a simple sprain, but it's going to hurt for a couple of weeks,' she warned him. 'You'll need to rest it for the next couple of days with ice to reduce the swelling, wrapped in some kind of cloth so it doesn't burn your skin. I'd suggest fifteen minutes of ice treatment per hour, but no more than three hours in total over the next twenty-four. You also need to use an elastic bandage from your toes to the middle of your lower leg, to support the sprain. And if you can put a couple of pillows on a chair and prop your ankle up so it's higher than your heart, it'll help it heal more quickly. If you've got some ibuprofen at home, that'd be best painkiller to use because it'll help reduce the swelling.' She smiled at him. 'If it's still giving you a lot of gyp tomorrow it might be worth going to the emergency department at St Piran's and ask them to take a look, but I'm pretty sure it's only a sprain rather than a fracture.'

'I know you from somewhere, don't I?' he asked.

'I'm a nurse at the Penhally Bay Surgery,' she said. 'And I'm the school liaison nurse.'

He nodded. 'That's where I've seen you—my boy's in Year Six. He's been nagging me lately about my lunchbox not being healthy enough and telling me to swap the cake for another piece of fruit.'

She laughed. 'Glad to hear the message is getting through.'

He moved, and gritted his teeth as pain clearly shot through him. 'Thanks for looking after me. You're here with Tom, aren't you?'

'I…um…' Flora couldn't help blushing. 'Yes.'

Ian smiled. 'He's a top bloke, our Tom.'

'Absolutely,' she agreed. 'Ian, I don't have an ice pack with me, but I do have an elastic bandage. I can at least strap up your ankle and get you to elevate it until you can get a lift home.'

A couple of the other football players helped him up and supported him over to his car; Ian called his wife on his mobile phone and asked her to get a taxi to the football ground and rescue him. Flora strapped up his ankle, made sure that he was comfortable, and then went back to watch the end of the match.

'What happened to Ian?' Tom asked when he came over to her at the end of the match.

'He sprained his ankle.'

Get 2 books Free!
Plus, receive a FREE mystery gift

If you have enjoyed reading this Medical romance story, then why not take advantage of this **FREE** book offer and we'll send you two more titles from this series absolutely **FREE**!

Accepting your **FREE** books and **FREE** mystery gift places you under no obligation to buy anything.

As a member of the Mills & Boon Book Club™ you'll receive your favourite Series books up to 2 months ahead of the shops, plus all these exclusive benefits:

- 🌹 FREE home delivery
- 🌹 Exclusive offers and our monthly newsletter
- 🌹 Membership to our special rewards programme

We hope that after receiving your free books you'll want to remain a member. But the choice is yours. So why not give us a go. You'll be glad you did!

Visit www.millsandboon.co.uk for the latest news and offers.

Mrs/Miss/Ms/Mr .... Initials ....

BLOCK CAPITALS PLEASE

Surname ....

Address ....

....

....

.... Postcode ....

Email ....

M1DIA

NO STAMP
NEEDED!

FREE BOOK OFFER

FREEPOST NAT 10298

RICHMOND

TW9 1BR

NO STAMP
NECESSARY
IF POSTED IN
THE U.K. OR N.I.

'Poor guy. It's going to make things difficult for him at work—he's a police officer.'

'He's going to be on desk duty for a few days, then,' Flora said.

'Did you enjoy the match, Joey?' Tom asked.

Joey nodded but his eyes were very dark. Tom and Flora exchanged a glance, guessing that the little boy was thinking of his dad. Tom crouched down. 'Hey. You played really well. And I bet your dad would have been really proud of you.'

Joey's bottom lip wobbled for a second, then he turned away.

Tom bit his lip, clearly thinking he'd made a mess of it.

Flora squeezed his hand and mouthed, 'You said the right thing. Don't blame yourself—just give him a moment.'

'We'd better go home and have a shower, because we're both covered in mud,' Tom said. 'And we have to be home for one, because Grandma said that's when lunch is going to be ready. She's cooking chicken, your favourite.'

'Is Flora coming?' Joey asked.

Flora hadn't been invited and had no intention of muscling in. After all, she was really just Tom's friend—acquaintance, really. She had no real connection to Kevin or to Susie.

Tom glanced at her, and she shook her head silently.

'No, we've already taken up her morning with the football. She has things to do round the farm. Come on, we'll drop her home and you can say hello to Banjo, and then we have to get going,' Tom said.

Before Flora knew it, she was home again, just her and the dog. Funny, a week ago that had been fine with her. Right now, it felt…empty.

Which was totally ridiculous.

She couldn't be falling for Tom—and Joey—that fast. Cross with herself, she made sure that she was busy for the rest of the day. Even so, the time dragged; the next morning dragged, too, because Tom was off duty and was taking Joey to school himself.

But at lunchtime she was catching up with paperwork in the surgery when her mobile phone rang.

'Hi. Are you busy tonight?' Tom asked.

'Not particularly,' Flora said. 'Why?'

'Because I'd like to invite you to dinner at my place. Joey tells me that he's enjoying cooking with you in the mornings, so he and I are going to be chefs. Is there anything you don't eat or you're allergic to?'

'No.'

'Great.' He gave her his address and directions. 'See you at six?'

'OK. Six it is.'

Flora felt ridiculously shy as she ended the call. This felt like a proper date—especially as it was Valentine's Day.

Valentine's Day.

Should she get Tom a card, or was that being a bit pushy? Was it too early in their relationship?

Oh, help. She was no good at this dating stuff. But on the way to Tom's flat, she dropped into the supermarket to buy a box of chocolates for Tom and Joey as a host gift and a huge display of cards caught her eye. She spent a while choosing one: nothing mushy, just a photograph of a simple heart-shaped box filled with chocolates. Sitting in her car, she simply wrote Tom's name inside it and signed it with two kisses; then she slipped the card into the envelope and put it in her handbag. She'd give it to him later, if she felt the moment was right.

Tom's flat was in a modern block on the first floor. She rang the doorbell, feeling ridiculously nervous.

He answered the door. 'Come in. Joey's just watching some cartoons. Can I take your coat?' He gave her a brief kiss hello as he took her coat, and her knees went weak. 'You look gorgeous,' he whispered. 'I love that colour on you.' She was wearing a black calf-length skirt and a teal-coloured top.

Colour seeped into her face. 'Thank you.' She strove for lightness. 'You don't look so bad yourself.' In dark trousers and a white shirt, he looked absolutely edible; she wanted to kiss him again, but at the same time she didn't want to seem pushy.

'Jojo, Flora's here,' he called.

Joey appeared from the living room. 'We made you dinner.'

'Thank you. And I brought you these as a gift.' She handed him the chocolates. 'Though they're for after dinner, OK?'

'Thank you.' Joey smiled at her. 'I made this at school.' He handed her an envelope.

'For me?'

He nodded.

When she opened it, there was a huge lump in her throat. The envelope contained a simple card with a heart shape cut out from red tissue paper. Inside, it said, *'To Flora from Joey'*, in very careful handwriting, and there were two kisses.

'That's lovely, Joey, and what beautiful handwriting.'

'We made cards at school.' He bit his lip, and she knew what he wasn't saying—that the children had all made them for their parents. 'I made one for Uncle Tom, too.'

She glanced at Tom and saw the sheen in his eyes; clearly the card had had a real emotional impact on him, too. She crouched down to Joey's level. 'This is the nicest card I've ever had. Can I give you a thank-you hug?'

Joey deliberated and she thought he was going to say no— then he nodded.

She hugged him. 'Thank you. And I'm going to put this on my fridge when I get home.'

'Can I watch cartoons again now?'

'Sure you can,' Tom said. 'I'm going to give Flora a guided

tour.' He showed her around the flat. 'Living room, obviously.' There were lots of photographs on the mantelpiece: an older couple that she assumed were his parents; a wedding picture that she guessed was Susie and Kevin, as there was another of the same couple with a baby; a picture of Tom with a much smaller Joey on his shoulders. There was one large bookcase crammed with books, and another crammed with films; she wasn't surprised to see a state-of-the-art games console next to his TV.

'Kitchen diner.' The kitchen was at one end and there was a table at the far end, by the window.

'Something smells nice,' she said.

'Bathroom, if you need it.' Plain, masculine and gleamingly clean, she noticed.

'And those two…' he gestured to the final two closed doors '…are my room and Joey's.'

'So where did you put Kevin's parents when they stayed?'

'My room, and I slept on the couch. It wasn't a big deal.' He glanced at his watch. 'Dinner's about ready. Would you like to go and sit down? Joey—time for dinner, sweetheart.'

Joey and Flora sat down at the kitchen table, and Tom brought in the meal.

'Chicken with cream and asparagus sauce. I'm impressed.'

'The sauce is from a packet,' Tom admitted with a smile. 'Joey, I take it you want ketchup with yours rather than my sauce?'

The little boy nodded.

Pudding turned out to be ice cream, out-of-season raspberries, and choc-chip cookies. 'Shop-bought, I'm afraid,' Tom confessed. 'I know they're not up to your standard.'

'They're still lovely, though—thank you. And I insist on doing the washing-up.'

Tom made them both a coffee, then ran a bath for Joey

while Flora made a start on the washing-up. She could hear a 'Hang on, I need to check it's not too hot before you get in—OK, safe now. Are there enough bubbles in there?' There was the sound of splashing, and then Tom reappeared, looking a bit damp.

'Joey's sense of humour,' he said.

She just laughed.

He came to stand behind her, wrapped his arms round her waist, and kissed the skin at the edge of the neckline of her top. 'You're adorable.'

'You're not so bad yourself, Tom Nicholson.' She twisted round slightly so she could kiss him. 'And that was a gorgeous meal.'

'Chicken, baked potatoes and vegetables? It wasn't exactly posh. Cooking isn't my strong point, but I'm trying.'

'It tasted good and it was a balanced meal,' she said. 'You're doing just fine.'

He kissed her again, then released her and picked up a tea-towel so he could start drying up. By the time they'd finished, Joey was ready to come out of the bath.

'Can I read you a bedtime story?' Flora asked.

Joey smiled, looking pleased, and found a story about a dog.

Tom joined them, sitting on the end of Joey's bed while Flora read. When it came to the part in the story where the dog talked, Tom did the voices and Joey's face lit up.

Flora kissed the little boy when she'd finished. 'Goodnight, sweetheart. Sleep well.'

Tom tucked his nephew in, and kissed him too. 'Goodnight, Jojo. See you in the morning.' Quietly, they left the room; she noticed that Tom left the door ajar and the landing light on.

'He gets bad dreams if it's dark,' Tom said. 'I put a night-light on when he's asleep, but he likes the light on in the landing while he's falling asleep.'

'Bless him.'

'Do you have to go yet, or will you come and sit with me for a while?' he asked.

'I'll stay,' she said.

He smiled, switched the light over from the main overhead lamp to an uplighter, and put some very quiet music on the stereo.

'I like this,' she said.

'It's good stuff to chill out to,' Tom told her. He scooped her onto his lap and kissed her; Flora, instead of worrying that she was squashing him, nestled closer, enjoying the closeness.

'I was touched that Joey made that card for me,' she said.

'He made the same one for me,' Tom said. 'When I opened it, I was so choked, I could hardly speak. And he actually let me hug him to say thank you.'

'It sounds as if he's made a decision to let you close.'

'I hope so. And he held my hand on the way to school today.' He paused. 'He said you told him he had to hold your hand between the car and school so you knew he was safe.' He swallowed hard. 'He said he wanted to know I was safe, too.'

'Oh, Tom—that's great.'

'If it hadn't been for you and Banjo I'd still be struggling. It's your warmth that's helped him open up to me,' he said. 'So I owe you.'

'You don't owe me anything.'

'Are you sure about that? I was kind of hoping to pay you in kisses.'

She smiled. 'Tom, you don't have to pay me.'

'Spoilsport,' he teased. 'Let me ask you another question.' He pulled her slightly closer and whispered in her ear, 'Will you be my Valentine, Flora Loveday?'

There was a huge lump in her throat; it was the kind of

question she'd never thought anyone would ask her, much less a man as beautiful as Tom Nicholas. 'Yes,' she whispered.

In answer, he kissed her. The kiss deepened, became more demanding, and, the next thing she knew, they were lying full length on the sofa, his body pressed against hers and leaving her in no doubt that he was aroused.

'I'm not going to push you into anything,' he said softly, his hand gliding along the curve of her bottom. 'I just wanted to lie with you in my arms.' He nudged the neckline of her top aside and rested his cheek against her shoulder. 'You smell of roses and vanilla. It makes me hungry.'

'What, after all the ice cream you ate tonight?' she teased.

He laughed. 'You make me hungry, Flora. And being with you...I don't know. You make me feel different. In a good way.'

They lay there quietly together, just holding each other and listening to the music. When the album finished, Tom went to check on Joey. 'He's asleep, bless him. I've just put his nightlight on.'

Shyness washed over Flora. 'I guess I ought to be going. Banjo needs his walk.'

'OK. Ring me when you get home, so I know you're home safely?'

It felt strange that someone was concerned about her; she was so used to just getting on and doing things by herself. It warmed her, too. 'Sure.'

'Before you go.' He handed her an envelope. 'Open it later.'

A Valentine's card? she wondered. She fished the card from her bag and handed it to him. 'For you,' she said shyly.

'Great minds think alike, hmm?' He kissed her lightly. 'Thank you, honey.'

'Open it later,' she said, not wanting him to open it in front of her.

'OK.' He paused. 'I'm doing show-and-tell with Joey tomorrow.'

'I thought you had a day off?' she asked, surprised.

'I am, but I'm still going to be there with the crew. I wouldn't miss it for the world. And I was wondering if you might be free for lunch tomorrow?'

It was a busy day, with surgery in the morning and then a postnatal class in the afternoon. 'It'd have to be a really quick one,' she said.

'Great—how about a picnic on the beach if it isn't raining?' He smiled. 'And we'll eat the picnic in my car if it's wet.'

'That'd be lovely.'

He kissed her goodbye at the door, his mouth sweet and soft and tempting. Desire and need flowed through her, and she kissed him back lingeringly.

When she got home, unable to resist any longer, she opened the envelope. The front of the card had a cartoon of a bee that had obviously flown in a heart shape, with the words 'bee my honey' written in the heart. Inside, Tom had written 'My adorable Flora' and signed it with two kisses. That was Tom all over, she thought: jokey and charming on the outside and keeping all the deep emotion inside.

She called him. 'I'm home.'

'Good. Did you open the card?'

'Yes.'

'Was it OK?'

'It was lovely, Tom.' She bit her lip. 'Sorry mine was a bit, well, drippy.'

'No. It was sweet. Like you.' His voice grew husky. 'Next time I eat a chocolate, I'm going to think about kissing you.' Heat spread through her at his words. 'See you tomorrow, honey.'

* * *

Her surgery the next morning was as she'd expected, apart from her ten-o'clock appointment, fifteen-year-old Emmy Kingston, who really should've been at school. 'Can Shelley stay with me?' Emmy asked, gesturing to her friend.

Emmy was guarding her stomach and the way she was standing made Flora think the worst. It wasn't her place to judge, but if her suspicion was right then the poor child would need all the support she could get. 'If you want her to stay with you, then that's fine.'

Emmy looked relieved, and accepted Flora's invitation to sit down.

'Tell me about it,' Flora said. 'How can I help you?'

'I've done something really stupid, and my parents are going to kill me.' Emmy bit her lip and a tear rolled down her face. 'I should've said no but I… It's so hard. And you're going to think…'

Flora reached out and squeezed her hand. 'I'm not going to think *anything*, sweetheart. I'm a nurse, and my job is to help you.'

'And you won't tell my mum and dad?'

'Your appointment is absolutely confidential,' Flora reassured her. 'It's between you and me, unless I think you're at risk of being hurt or abused. The important thing is that you're protected, OK?'

Another tear rolled down Emmy's cheek.

'Show her, Em,' Shelley said, patting her shoulder.

Gingerly, Emmy lifted up her top to reveal—not quite what Flora had expected. The girl had a pierced navel and the area around the piercing was bright red and swollen; there was a yellowish discharge from her belly button.

'That looks really painful,' Flora said. 'How long has it been like that?'

'I had it done on Saturday. Mum and Dad said I wasn't allowed to, so I didn't tell them I was doing it. I had a sleepover at Shelley's so they wouldn't see.' Emmy's voice wobbled. 'I wish I hadn't done it now.'

'It looks to me as if it's infected. It's quite common to get a bacterial infection with a piercing—have you managed to keep it dry over the last three days?'

Emmy nodded. 'That's what the piercer said, don't wash it even with salt water or it might get infected. I did everything he said.'

'You've just been a bit unlucky,' Flora said. 'I want to take your temperature—sometimes these infections can turn really nasty, and I want to be sure you're not developing septicaemia or something really scary. Is that OK?'

Emmy gave her consent, and Flora checked the girl's temperature. 'The good news is that we've caught the infection in time—your temperature's fine. You'll need some antibiotic cream to clear up the infection and stop it hurting, and if it doesn't start getting better by Friday you'll need to come back and see the doctor to get some antibiotic tablets.' She quickly tapped information into the computer. 'Try not to touch your belly button or pick at it, in the meantime.'

'It hurts too much to touch it,' Emmy said ruefully.

'Antibiotics will help with that,' Flora reassured her. 'It might be worth taking some paracetamol as well. Dr Lovak will sign the prescription for you when he's seen his next patient, if you don't mind waiting in the reception area for a few minutes?'

Emmy exhaled sharply. 'So it's going to be all right?'

'Yes.'

'See? I told you,' Shelley said, hugging her shoulders.

'And you're not going to tell my mum?'

'No,' Flora said, 'but I think you should.'

Emmy shook her head. 'I can't. Mum will go *mad*.'

'When you came in,' Flora told her gently, 'the way you were standing and holding your tummy, I thought you might be pregnant. I wouldn't mind betting your mum's thinking the same thing and she's worried sick about you—especially as my guess is that you've been avoiding her since Saturday.'

'I have,' Emmy admitted, biting her lip.

'Then talk to her tonight,' Flora advised quietly. 'Yes, she might shout at you for going against her wishes, but she'll want to know that you're all right.'

'She'll make me take it out.'

'That's not a good idea until the infection's cleared up—it needs to be able to drain and make sure that an abscess doesn't form. You can always tell her to ring me if she wants some reassurance,' Flora said.

Emmy's lower lip wobbled. 'Thank you so much.'

Flora patted her shoulder. 'A couple more days and you'll feel a lot better, I promise. But if you don't, come back and see Dr Lovak. We're here to help you, not shout at you or judge you, OK?'

'OK.' Emmy rubbed the tears away with the back of her hand, and let her friend shepherd her out to the reception area.

Flora had just seen her last patient and was finishing typing up her notes when her phone beeped. It was a text from Tom: *'Am in the car park whenever you're ready.'*

'On my way', Flora texted back, and went out to meet him.

He greeted her with a kiss.

'How did show-and-tell go?' she asked.

'Unbelievable.' Tom's eyes glittered. 'I actually saw Joey nudge the boy next to him and say, "That's my Uncle Tom." He sounded really proud.'

'That's because he *is* proud of you, Tom.' She hugged him. 'Well done, you.'

'How was your morning?' he asked.

'Busy, but good.'

He kissed her again. 'When do you need to be back?'

She glanced at her watch. 'In forty-five minutes.'

'Right—beach it is.' He drove them down to the car park by the beach; he had a picnic rug in the back of the car, along with a flask of hot chocolate and a bag from the deli containing sandwiches and fruit.

Flora enjoyed just being with him, having a leisurely lunch and then sitting on the rug with his arms wrapped round her, listening to the sea and the shrieks of the gulls.

'This is a perfect day,' he said softly, resting his cheek against her hair. 'Being with Joey this morning, and being with you right now. And you're definitely the silver lining in the school fire—I wouldn't have met you, if it hadn't happened.' He drew her closer. 'And I'm really glad I've met you, Flora.'

'I'm glad I've met you, too.' With Tom in her world, everything seemed so much brighter. Crazy—and no way would she admit that to him, not yet—but it was true. Tom made her feel special. As if she mattered.

'So when am I going to see you again?' he asked when he'd driven her back to the surgery.

'I have tomorrow off, if you want to do something.'

He looked sombre. 'Could I ask you something?'

'Sure.'

'The other day, you said you'd help if I wanted to go through Susie's things...'

'And I meant what I said. Of course I'll help.' She stroked his face. 'Are you sure you're ready for it, Tom?'

'No, and I'm not sure I'll ever be ready,' he admitted, 'but it has to be done.'

'It's better to do it with someone else,' she said softly. 'I had help and it got me through one of the hardest days ever.'

He hugged her. 'Thank you. Can I pick you up when I've taken Joey to school?'

'Absolutely.' She kissed him. 'And, Tom?'

'Yes?'

'Try not to brood about it. Yes, it'll be tough, but you won't be on your own. See you tomorrow.'

CHAPTER EIGHT

On Wednesday morning, Tom picked Flora up after he'd taken Joey to school, looking very sombre. For once, his car stereo was silent, and the grim set of his jaw told Flora that he wasn't in the mood for conversation, either.

He parked outside one of the cottages near the cliffs, and she noticed his hand was shaking as he opened the front door. He took a deep breath when he stepped inside, then leaned his head back against the wall and closed his eyes. 'I hate this. It feels so wrong.'

'I know.' She took his hand and held it, willing him to take strength from her nearness.

'Clearing out their house makes everything seem so final.' He swallowed hard. 'I suppose I was leaving it in the hope that it was all a bad dream and they'd come back—but they're not coming back, are they?'

'No, Tom, they're not,' she said, as gently as she could.

'It's such a waste. Such a bloody waste. There are people out there who hurt others, who lie and cheat and make people miserable, and they seem to swan through life without any worries. And people like my sister and her husband, people who were kind and always helped others…' He shook his head in anguish. 'It's not fair. Why did they have to die?'

There was no answer to that. All she could do was hold his hand.

A muscle worked in his jaw. 'OK. I'm pulling myself to-gether. Let's do this.' Then he looked completely lost. 'How do you go about packing up someone's life?'

This was something she could help with. Something she'd been through herself. 'You think of the good times,' she told him. 'You keep the nice memories as you go. And you have boxes. One for things to go to the charity shop, one for things you want to keep—even if you're not up to dealing with them yet, like photo albums—and one for things you're going to throw out.' She paused. 'You don't have to do it all at once, Tom. We can do just one room at a time, if it makes it easier on you.'

He shook his head. 'It needs to be done, and I've organised for the council to come and take the furniture to help families that need rehoming.' He took a deep breath. 'Part of me thinks I ought to move in here and give Joey some continuity. But I just *can't*, Flora. I can't live here with all these memories. They'll suffocate me.'

'Joey will understand when he's older,' she reassured him. 'He has a new life now and it'll be easier for him to get used to that if he lives with you away from here.'

He nodded. 'We'll do the hard stuff first. Bedroom.'

Flora helped him take the clothes out of the wardrobe and pack them into bags he was planning to take to the charity shop. 'Maybe you could to keep something for Joey—his dad's favourite sweater or his mum's favourite dress,' she suggested. 'Something personal for him, for the future.'

'Yeah, you're right.'

Tom's face was set. Grim. She knew this was ripping him to shreds inside, and yet he was trying so hard not to show any emotion.

The kitchen was next; it was easy to pack up, because there was nothing really personal there. Except for the outside of the fridge, photographs and postcards and little notes held on with magnets. Tom stripped those and put them in the 'deal with later' pile.

When they started to pack up the living room, the strain was really etched on his face. Books, music, photograph albums... She could practically see the tension radiating from his body.

And then he picked up a photograph from the mantelpiece. His hand shook, and he dropped it; she heard a crack as the glass smashed. Reaching down to deal with it, Tom sucked in a breath, and she saw red blooming over his hand.

'Kitchen. Now.' She made him stand under the light so she could check the cut for fragments of glass, then cleaned the wound and put a pad on it. 'Press on it. It'll staunch the flow,' she said. 'And I'll get rid of the broken glass.'

'I'll do it.'

'Tom, I want you to sit there for three minutes, and that's a medical order,' she said, taking an old newspaper into the living room. She wrapped the broken glass in some newspaper, then turned the frame over. She could see why he'd dropped the frame; the photograph was of Tom himself, with his sister and Joey, looking incredibly happy.

Memories.

Sometimes the good ones were the ones that hurt you most. She'd found it hard to look at her parents' photographs for the first couple of months, feeling the loss ripping through her again every time she saw them.

Gently, she removed the photograph from the broken frame and slid it inside one of the photograph albums to keep it safe. Then she wrapped up the broken frame and took the two parcels into the kitchen. 'All done,' she said quietly.

'Sorry. It just...' His voice caught.

She held him close. 'I know. I've been there myself. Come on. I think it's time we took a break. Let's go back to mine for lunch.'

Back at the farmhouse, she took a jug of home-made vegetable soup from the fridge and heated it, then set it on the table along with cheese, butter and some rolls she'd bought at the bakery the day before.

Tom pushed his plate away untouched. 'Flora, I'm sorry to be rude—I don't think I can possibly eat.'

'Yes, you can; and, yes, you will.'

'I feel too choked.'

Remembering how Kate Tremayne had chivvied her, and how she'd appreciated it later, she refused to let him give in. 'You need to keep up your strength, for Joey's sake. Listen, Tom, I didn't really know your sister, so I can't imagine what she'd say in this situation—but if she loved you as much as you loved her, I'm pretty sure she would've wanted you to remember the good times and celebrate her, not mourn her.'

Tom dragged in a breath. 'Yes, she loved me—even though I drove her crazy when I was a teenager. And I loved her. I would've done anything to spare her what happened, Flora. And Kevin—he wasn't just an in-law I had to tolerate for Susie's sake. I really liked him. You know they say you can't choose your family? Well, he was the kind of bloke I would've chosen to have as my family.'

'I know what you mean. But you still have Joey, and they'll both live on in him,' she said softly. 'You'll see them in his face as they grow up—and there will come a day, Tom, when you can talk to him about them without it hurting. You'll be able to tell him how much they loved him and how proud they'd be of how he's growing up.'

He closed his eyes. 'Right now, it doesn't feel like it.'

'Of course not, because you're not there yet. Trust me, it'll come—you'll still get days when you wake up and you know there's a big empty space in your life and you want to howl, but it gets easier to deal with as time passes.'

He opened his eyes again and looked at her. 'Is it like that for you?'

She nodded. 'Sometimes one of my dad's favourite records will come on the radio, or I'll smell my mum's perfume in a department store, and it still chokes me inside—but it's getting easier. It just takes time and you need to be a bit less hard on yourself. Let people close to you, Tom, and they'll help you.'

'I do let people close to me.'

She said nothing, just stroked his face and gave him a sad little smile.

Tom thought about it later that evening. Was Flora right? Did he let people close to him? Or did he use all the terrible jokes and puns that were his stock-in-trade at work to keep people at bay?

The more he thought about it, the more he started to realise that Flora had a point. He *didn't* let people that close. And, if he thought about it, he could trace it right back to when Ben had died. The first person he'd really lost, his best friend, and yet he'd never even visited Ben's grave. He'd withdrawn a bit after Ben had died, until his mum had talked about taking him to see the doctor; and then he'd realised that if he didn't start smiling and laughing, she really would take him to see someone. He hadn't wanted that kind of fuss. So he'd started telling silly jokes, smiled all the time, and driven Susie to distraction with practical jokes. But he'd never really let anyone close again. He'd kept everything on the surface.

Which was one of the reasons he was struggling to be a stand-in dad to his nephew, because he didn't have a clue what he was meant to do, how he was meant to feel.

And the more he thought about it, the more it worried him. Because he was starting to let Flora and Joey a lot closer than he was really comfortable with—and it scared him. Not because he was scared of being close to them, as such, more because he was scared of letting them down in the worst possible way. His job was dangerous—and he knew firefighters who hadn't made it. People who'd left grieving families behind.

Was that why he'd never let his relationships get too serious? And why he was struggling so hard to be a stand-in dad to Joey? Because he didn't want to leave a gaping hole in people's lives, and Joey had already lost so much?

He lay awake for a long, long time—and right at that moment he really could do with Flora in his arms. He needed her quiet strength, her warmth to comfort him. And that scared him even more. He'd never felt as if he'd needed a girlfriend before. He'd enjoyed female company, had fun with a carefree bachelor lifestyle…but this was different. Flora was nothing like the women he usually dated. She was quieter, more serious. She had depth.

And that made her incredibly dangerous. With her shy smile and her beautiful soft brown eyes and the sheer warmth she exuded—there was a real possibility that she could steal his heart. And break it.

Tom was still brooding about it on Thursday morning, when he dropped Joey at Flora's for breakfast. And he brooded all morning through inspection and cleaning the equipment, until the Tannoy warbled.

'Turnout, vehicle 54. Person fallen in river, Penhally Bay.'

This could be nasty, Tom thought. The cold snap had lasted a while now, so the water would be very cold and there was a real risk of the victim developing hypothermia. If the river was running swiftly, even if they managed to cling on to a branch or a rock, the current might pull them away and send them downstream,

He headed to the engine with the rest of the crew. Bazza

was in the driving seat and Steve was checking the computer. 'It was called in by mobile phone,' he said. 'So details are a bit sketchy—hopefully they'll call back with more information.'

Halfway to the village, Steve's mobile rang. 'Yup—uh-huh. Thanks.' He ended the call. 'It turns out it isn't a person in the river, it's a dog.'

Tom had come across this kind of thing before. 'Please tell me the owner hasn't tried to jump in and save the dog,' he said.

'No, the owner's an elderly man. He was walking by the river when he slipped on the ice and fell. Apparently he might have broken his hip—the ambulance is on its way. When he fell, the dog plunged down the bank and ended up in the river. The poor guy's frantic, but in too much pain to move.'

'Hopefully we can rescue the dog before the paramedics whisk him off to St Piran's,' Tom said. 'Walkway, ladder or rope, do you think?'

'We'll know as soon as we see it,' Steve said.

Even without the co-ordinates, they would've been able to see the site straight away, as the ambulance was already there. As Tom got out of the fire engine, he could see the paramedics gently lifting an elderly man onto a stretcher. The man was clearly distressed, calling, 'No, no! I can't go until Goldie's safe.'

Tom walked over to him. 'I'm Tom Nicholson—and I'm going to rescue your dog,' he said. 'Her name's Goldie?'

The elderly man was in tears. 'She fell down the bank. It's my fault. I slipped, and I caught her as I fell. She's like me, not so steady on her pins.' He choked on a sob. 'She's been in the water for ages. She's too old to cope with it. I've killed her.'

'No, you haven't,' Tom reassured him. 'Dogs are far more

resilient than you'd believe. Hang on in there, and I'll get her back for you.'

As soon he looked over the river bank, he could see that the elderly yellow Labrador was stuck against a branch and was clearly getting tired.

'Has anyone called the local vet ready to treat Goldie when I get her out?' he asked the crowd of bystanders.

'I'll go—they're just round the corner,' one man said.

'Thanks. And if someone could get a towel or a blanket to wrap her in?' He turned back to the crew. 'I'll go. It's going to be quickest if you rope me. The dog's too big for a tube—' the crew had tubes they could scoop smaller animals into and lift to safety '—so we'll get a rope round her, too, and I'll lift her.'

Slowly, knowing that his crew had the rope and could stop him falling if he slipped, he made his way down the bank to the dog.

'Goldie,' he called softly, 'hang on in there. I'll get you back to your family.' He knew the dog couldn't understand what he was saying, but he hoped the tone of his voice would reassure her and calm her.

'There's a good girl. Not long now. I'm just going to put the rope round you.' He'd just got the rope round her when there was a loud crack and the branch broke. The sound terrified the already frightened dog, who reacted by sinking her teeth into Tom's arm.

It hurt like mad, but he swallowed the yell, knowing it would panic the dog even more and earn him a second bite. 'OK, Goldie,' he said through gritted teeth. 'There's a good girl. Nearly there.'

The dog struggled in his arms, but he had her roped safely.

But, with his arms full of wet, tired, heavy dog, there was

no way he was going to be able to make it up the slippery bank on his own. 'I've got her. Haul me up,' Tom called up.

Slowly, slowly, the team hauled him up.

A flash popped in his face as he reached the top, the dog in his arms.

'Oh, for pity's sake,' he said, frowning. 'You can have your story in a minute. We need to get this dog treated, first.'

'Absolutely right,' Melinda Lovak, the local vet, said crisply. She crouched down and wrapped a towel round the shivering dog. 'Well done for bringing her out,' she said to Tom. Tenderly, she dried the dog. 'Hello, Goldie. Not the best time of year to go for a swim, is it?' she asked.

The dog looked slightly less frightened, clearly knowing the vet.

'There's a good girl,' Melinda said softly. Swiftly, she checked the animal over. 'Looks like you're going to be fine after your dip. Let's go and tell Bob, shall we?'

There was a faint wag of the tail.

'Bob, she's absolutely fine,' Melinda told the elderly man in the ambulance. 'Look, you can see her. The fireman got her out and she's wagging her tail.'

'The dog can't come in the ambulance, love,' the paramedic told her.

'What's going to happen to her?' Bob asked. 'I live on my own. I can't go to the hospital, I need to stay with Goldie.'

'Yes, you can, because you need to be treated,' Melinda said. 'Don't worry about her. I'll take her back to the surgery with me. Dragan and the boys won't mind if we have another dog for a few days—or, if Goldie decides she doesn't like it with Bramble at our place, Lizzie Chamberlain at the kennels will take her in until you're back on your feet.'

Bob was almost in tears. 'Thank you—I don't know what I'd do without her.' He looked at Tom. 'And thank you. You saved her life.'

'That's what I'm here for,' Tom said simply. 'I'm glad she's all right.'

'She'll be absolutely fine,' Melinda reassured Bob. 'Now go and get yourself fixed, OK? I'll ring the hospital later to let you know how Goldie's doing.'

The paramedic closed the door and the ambulance headed off to St Piran's.

Tom's arm was throbbing; wincing, he rolled up his sleeve to look at it.

'You need to get that looked at,' Melinda said.

Tom shrugged. 'It's not that bad. I'm fine.'

'Trust me,' she said with a smile, 'I've been bitten enough in my time. That's a puncture wound, so it could get infected—and you probably need a tetanus jab.'

He grimaced. 'Oh, great.'

She laughed, 'A big fireman like you, scared of a little needle? Don't be such a baby!' she teased. 'The doctor's surgery is just over there and it'll take ten minutes, tops.' She made a fuss of the dog. 'And I'd better get this one in the warm. Come on, girl.'

'You've had your orders,' Steve said with a grin. 'And she's a vet. She knows what she's talking about.'

'And can I interview you now?' the reporter asked.

'Look, it was just a routine rescue. No big deal,' Tom said.

The reporter smiled at him. 'But our readers love this sort of story. It's a feel-good story, perfect to lift people's spirits at a miserable time of year.'

'I…' He sighed. 'OK. As long as you put something in there about keeping your dog on a lead when you're walking by an icy river, and calling the emergency services rather than risking your own safety—in this kind of weather, you can get into difficulties really quickly and it means the emergency services have to do twice the amount of work, rescuing you as well as your pet.'

'I'll make sure I put that in,' the reporter said. She glanced down at his left hand and clearly saw that he wasn't wearing a wedding ring. 'Actually, maybe I can take you for a coffee? You must be freezing.'

'He's going to the doctor's to get his arm seen to, love,' Steve put in.

'I can interview you while you're waiting to be seen,' the reporter said with a smile, 'and then maybe we can go for a coffee afterwards.'

Tom didn't want to go for coffee with anyone except Flora; though they were keeping things to themselves, right now, and he wasn't going to make life awkward for her by giving a declaration in front of half of Penhally. 'Mmm,' he said noncommittally.

He had no idea if Flora was in surgery this morning or if she was working at one of the schools, and suppressed the hope that she might be the one to patch him up. And he still had to give the reporter a story. Feeling embarrassed, he went up to the reception desk, explained what had happened, and asked if someone could fit him in.

'Sit down, and we'll call you as soon as the nurse is free,' the receptionist said with a smile.

The reporter wasn't budging. 'So how did you feel when you saw the dog?'

'The same as the rest of the crew—we wanted to get her back safely on dry land, and reassure her owner so that he'd let the paramedics treat him,' Tom said. 'Look, there isn't much of a story. We simply responded to an emergency call.'

'But the dog was heavy. And it bit you.'

'The dog was cold, tired and frightened. She didn't mean to hurt me.'

'And the bite won't put you off rescuing the next dog?'

'Of course not. It's my job,' Tom said firmly.

'OK.' She finished scribbling notes on her pad. 'Shall we go for that coffee anyway?'

'Sorry, I have to get back to work,' Tom said.

She took a business card from her handbag. 'If you think of anything else, give me a call. Actually, it'd be nice to run a few features on the local emergency services. Maybe I can come and shadow you for a day.'

Something in her eyes told Tom that she didn't have just business in mind. And his suspicion was confirmed when she added, 'And, since you can't make that coffee, maybe I can take you out for a drink to say thanks for your help.'

The reporter was pretty; three months ago, Tom might've accepted the invitation. But things were very different now. 'That'd be nice. I'll have to check when my partner's free,' he said.

'Your partner?'

Three months ago, those words might've made him run a mile. But now...now, it was different. 'I assume the invitation extends to her, too?' Tom said, knowing full well that it wouldn't.

'I, um, sure. Of course.'

His name flashed up on the board above the reception desk. 'Sorry, I need to go.'

'Sure. Catch you later,' she said, and Tom had a pretty fair idea that she wouldn't call him at all.

To his mingled pleasure and embarrassment, it turned out that the nurse on duty was Flora.

She looked worried when he walked into her treatment room. 'What's happened? Are you all right?'

'I rescued a dog from the river, and she bit me.'

'Right, let me take a look—whose dog was it?'

'I didn't catch his last name. His first name's Bob. He's quite elderly, and the dog's a yellow Labrador called Goldie.'

'I know who you mean. Bob Thurston. Is he all right?'

'He slipped on the ice—the paramedics were worried enough to take him to St Piran's, so my guess is that he's probably broken something. Goldie slid down the bank and into the river. Luckily she was swept against a branch and stuck there, otherwise who knows how far she could've ended up downstream.'

'And she bit you? But Goldie's really gentle.'

'She was scared. It's not a big deal.'

'Does it hurt?'

'A bit,' he admitted. 'It throbs more than anything.'

'OK. Let me take a look—I want to make sure there isn't any damage to the structures beneath the bite, tendons and what have you. Is Goldie OK?'

'The vet's taken her back to the surgery. She says she'll look after her.'

Flora smiled. 'That's Melinda all over—she's lovely like that. She helped me find some homes when one of the feral farm cats had a litter. Jess Carmichael at the hospital—well, Jess Corezzi now she's married—took a couple, too.' She finished examining his arm. 'That looks fine,' she said. 'Tom, is your tetanus up to date?'

'I think so.'

'Mind if I check?' She looked up his record. 'It is. So you're safe from having a big fat needle in your arm.'

'Pity,' Tom said. 'I could've asked you to kiss it better.'

'You wish.'

'So how about it?' he asked.

'That depends on how brave you are while I sort this out.' She gave him a local anaesthetic, cleaned the wound, making sure there were no foreign bodies in it, and debrided some of tissue. 'I'm not going to stitch this,' she said, 'because it's a puncture wound, and you're more likely to get an infection if

I close it. And you do need antibiotics to be on the safe side, so I'll ask the doctor to write you a prescription.'

'OK. Do I get my kiss for being brave now?'

'Tom, I'm at work and so are you. I have patients waiting,' she protested. But she gave him a swift kiss.

'Would that be on account?' he asked hopefully.

She rolled her eyes. 'Yes. Go and rescue someone.'

'I'd rather scoop you up in a fireman's lift and take you somewhere quiet,' Tom said. He stole another kiss. 'But I'll do that later. Thanks for patching me up.'

'It's what I do,' she said with a smile.

When Tom had finished his shift, he drove to Flora's farmhouse to pick up Joey.

'How's your arm?' she asked.

'Sore,' he admitted, 'but it's OK.'

Joey looked worried. 'What's wrong with your arm?'

'I rescued a dog today—she fell in the river and got stuck. She was a bit worried when I rescued her,' Tom explained, 'and dogs can't tell you in words that they're scared, so she bit me. She didn't mean to hurt me, she was just frightened.'

'I know the dog,' Flora said. 'She's really quiet and soft, normally—she's quite old, too. She's a yellow Labrador called Goldie.'

'And she's doing absolutely fine,' Tom added. 'I rang the vet before the surgery closed, to see how she was. I'm fine, too, Jojo. Flora cleaned me up and put a dressing on, and I've got some special tablets so I don't get an infection in the wound.'

'So you rescued Uncle Tom,' Joey said to Flora.

'I was just doing my job—like he was doing his,' Flora said with a smile. 'Actually, I had to do a rescue myself today. This cold snap really seems to be knocking everyone for six. Young Jane Hallet in Year Four fell over in the playground at lunchtime and broke her arm, poor thing. I was there so

I could give her a painkiller and put her arm in a sling to make her more comfortable, but her mum had to take her to the emergency department in St Piran's. Luckily it happened just after her mum Marina finished her shift in the kitchen, so Marina was able to take her. I'll drop in to see them tomorrow on my way back from lunch and see how she is.'

'So what were you doing today?' Tom asked.

'Healthy eating with the Year Sixes—one of the girls has just been diagnosed as a diabetic, so we were talking about sugar and how the body processes it. I have a quiz so they can guess how many teaspoons of sugar are in each item.' She smiled at him. 'Guess how many teaspoons of sugar there are in a can of fizzy drink?'

'The non-diet sort, I assume?' Tom asked.

'Uh-huh.'

He thought about it. 'Five?' he guessed.

'Too low. Joey?' she prompted.

'Seven?' the little boy suggested.

'Closer—but still too low. Believe it or not, it's nine,' she told them. 'That's why they're really bad for teeth. We did some experiments with eggshells in different sorts of drink so the children could see what effect the drinks would have on their teeth.'

'Eggshells being made of the same sort of stuff as teeth?' Tom asked.

'Exactly. Anyway, when they saw which ones dissolved, it's made a few of them think that maybe water's the best drink you can have.' She smiled at Joey. 'I'll do that with your class when you're in Year Six. But I'm going to be doing germs and super-soap with your class after half-term. And we might do the eggshell thing too, if you think it sounds like fun.'

Joey nodded enthusiastically.

'Ah, so you like science? Excellent. We can do some kitchen experiments,' Flora said. 'I know how to make a volcano.'

Joey beamed. 'That's cool.'

'Hey, can I be in on this?' Tom asked. 'And I know an experiment about how to make a plastic bottle into a rocket.'

'This sounds like a very half-term kind of thing to do,' Flora said. 'And I've heard the mums at school talking about that new science museum just up the coast. They say it's really good.'

'I think we need to go,' Tom said. 'What do you think, Joey?'

The little boy nodded.

'Then it's a date. Flora, is there any chance you can have a day off, next week, and come with us?' Tom asked.

'I'll check at work tomorrow to see if I can swap a shift with someone,' Flora said. 'Given that I won't be doing my usual school sessions, I should be able to get a day off.'

'Cool,' Joey said, smiling at both of them.

CHAPTER NINE

ON FRIDAY, Flora dropped Joey at school and spent the morning working at the high school, doing a couple of talks about healthy eating and one about sexual health. During her lunch break, she drove out to Chyandour Farm on the outskirts of Penhally to see how Lizzie was doing.

As she reached the end of the drive, she saw the fire engines there; water was being sprayed onto one of the barns.

Tom came over to her as she climbed out of the car. 'Just the woman we could do with.'

'What's happened?'

'The lower barn caught fire. John rang us, then tried to beat out the flames, but he burned his arm. Can you take a look?'

'Sure.' She grabbed her medical kit from the car, then followed Tom to where John Hallet was standing. She persuaded him to go and sit down in the kitchen so she could take a look at his injuries properly and treat him.

'I only popped in to see how Lizzie was doing—I wasn't expecting to treat you, too,' she said wryly.

'They say things come in threes,' John said. 'Let's just hope they don't!'

She looked at his arm. 'I'm relieved to say the burns are pretty superficial. If it had been your hands, I would have sent you to St Piran's, but I can dress this for you. Have you taken anything for the pain?'

'Not yet.'

She gave him a painkiller, then cleaned and dressed the burn. 'So how's Lizzie doing?'

'She wants to be back at school, but Marina had to take her to St Piran's to have her cast on today. She'll be fine,' John said. 'Nicola's home with a headache. I'll get her to come down and put the kettle on and make tea for everyone.'

Nicola Hallet was the quiet one in the family, Flora remembered, the only one who wasn't sporty or glamorous. Her older sisters Stacey and Keeley were both model-thin and stunning, popular with all the girls in the village and drooled over by the boys; young Lizzie was into tap-dancing and gymnastics and athletics, and was always talking about how her older brother Jonathan was the captain of the football team at the primary school last year and had a purple belt in kick-boxing. And she had a feeling that Nicola had a pretty hard time fitting in.

'If she's got a headache, she's probably better resting. I can make the tea,' she offered.

'No, she'll do it. She's been that mardy, lately.' John called up to her, and a minute or so later Nicola came downstairs into the kitchen.

'We need some tea for the firefighters, love,' John said.

Nicola nodded and filled the kettle with water.

'How's your headache?' Flora asked.

Nicola shrugged. 'It'll go.'

'Have you taken anything for it?'

Nicola shrugged again. 'I will in a bit.'

Flora looked at the girl, wondering. Nicola had always been a bit on the plump side, but she'd definitely put on weight since Flora had last seen her—and she was trying to hide it with baggy clothes. Remembering her own teenage years, how she'd felt she didn't fit in and had cheered herself up with chocolate biscuits, Flora wondered if Nicola might be worried about something and comfort-eating as a way of dealing with it. Not that she'd ask the girl in front of her dad.

'Let me give you a hand with the tea, Nicola,' she offered. 'John, if you can do us a favour and find out who takes sugar?'

'Will do,' he said.

As soon as he'd closed the door, Flora asked gently, 'Is everything all right, Nicola?'

'I'm fine. Just fine,' Nicola said. 'It's only a headache.'

Flora was pretty sure it was more than just a headache making the girl miserable. 'You're not having any problems at school?'

'Why should I be?'

'No reason,' Flora said quietly. 'I just remember that it's hard being a teenager, that's all. And sometimes people make it harder for you.'

Nicola just shrugged, and concentrated on putting tea leaves in the pot.

'If you ever need anyone to talk to, you know you can always come and see me at the drop-in clinic at school. Or at the surgery. Anything you say will be just between you and me, OK?'

For a moment, Flora thought that the girl was going to say something—but then the kitchen door opened and John walked back in. Any chance that Nicola would confide in her vanished instantly.

She didn't get a chance to talk to Nicola when the tea had been handed round, either, because the girl had disappeared back to her room. And Flora was due back in the surgery for the afternoon, so she had to get on. 'If you're in pain or you see any sign of infection, John, don't be stubborn about it—come and see us at the surgery.'

'I'll be fine.'

John was of the old school—and that meant he'd only see the doctor if he was in so much pain that he couldn't sleep. 'As long as you know that the sooner we look at a problem, the quicker it is to fix it,' she said gently. 'Don't be too proud or too stubborn.'

'All right, love,' he said.

After surgery that afternoon, Flora picked Joey up from school as usual, and made dinner with him. When Tom arrived after his shift, he gave her a hello hug and ruffled Joey's hair; Flora was pleased that the little boy didn't pull away.

While Joey played with Banjo, Flora made coffee for herself and Tom.

'Flora, are you busy next weekend?' Tom asked.

She was never busy. Not that she wanted him to think she was completely desperate. 'I'm not doing anything important. Why?'

'It's the football league dinner—kind of a late Valentine's ball sort of thing. We have it every year. It's the local emergency services league, so all the teams have a table—fire crews, the police and the medics—and we take our partners with us. The fire crew team has a huge rivalry thing going on with the medics, but it's all in good fun and—well, I know it's a bit late notice, but I wasn't even sure if I was going to go this year, the way things were. But my parents are going to be here next weekend and they're more than happy to babysit for us, if you'd like to come to the dinner with me?'

He wanted her to go to a posh do with him? Help. She never got invited to posh dos like this. She didn't have a thing to wear, or a clue where to find something suitable. And if it was the same crowd as the football lot, who were incredibly cliquey, she wasn't sure she wanted to be there. 'Um, can I think about it?'

He looked slightly hurt, but shrugged. 'Sure. Can I ask you something else?'

She spread her hands. 'Of course.'

'My parents are coming over from France for a week or so. They're staying for a long weekend, then visiting Mum's brother, and then they're coming back next weekend. So I was wondering…will you come to dinner at my place tomorrow night to meet them?'

Asking her to a formal dinner as his date was one thing, but now he was asking her to meet his parents. As his friend—or as his girlfriend?

'I…um…' Oh, help. This situation was way outside what she was used to.

'They're nice, my parents. And they said they'd like to meet you.'

His parents knew about her? What had he said? Had he told them that she was Joey's babysitter, or that he was seeing her?

'Please?' he added.

How could she resist the appeal in his gorgeous dark eyes? 'All right.'

'Great. It'll be a proper home-cooked dinner. About six?'

Which meant it'd be early enough for Joey to be eating with them, she guessed. 'Sure. I'll be there.'

'I'd better get back,' he said. 'They'll be here in an hour or so.' He looked at Joey. 'Want a fireman's lift to the car?'

Joey's eyes brightened. 'Cool,' he said.

Tom looked delighted that Joey was finally opening up to him again, returning to their old rough-and-tumble relationship, and hoisted his nephew over his shoulder. But Flora noticed his wince of pain. She slipped her coat on and followed them out to the car. When Tom had strapped Joey into the car seat and closed the door, she said, 'Is your arm hurting you?'

'No.' But he didn't meet her eye.

'Tom?'

He shook his head. 'It's nothing. Just a bruise.'

Not his arm, then. And the fact he wasn't telling her straight made her suspicious. 'Where?'

'My back.'

'And you did that rescuing Goldie?'

He flapped a dismissive hand. 'Look, I'm fine.'

'Tom,' she said warningly.

He rolled his eyes. 'OK. There was another fire this afternoon. A little girl was stuck in her bedroom. Just as I got her out, the roof collapsed and a beam caught my shoulder. I'm fine.'

Flora's eyes narrowed. 'The roof collapsed.'

'Yes, but it missed me. Well, most of it missed me. And the little girl's absolutely fine.'

There was something he wasn't telling her. He was an experienced firefighter. He would've known if the structure was dangerous and the roof was likely to cave in—and yet he'd gone in anyway. And she remembered what he'd told her when he'd spoken about Ben. *I almost never lose anyone. I remember how it was for his parents...I don't want anyone else to go through that.*

And so he took risks. More risks, she thought, than anyone else on his crew would take. Reckless, even, because he didn't think of his own safety.

'Was anyone else with you?' she asked.

'No, they were putting out the fire.'

'So you went into a burning building, on your own, to rescue someone. You could've been killed.'

He frowned. 'Flora, it's my job. What was I meant to do, let her burn?'

'She was stuck in her bedroom. You could've put a ladder at the window or something, so you didn't have to go through the dangerous bit of the building to rescue her.'

'What I did was quicker.'

Maybe—but it was also something else. Something that really worried her. And it had to be said. 'And r-reckless.'

Tom lifted his chin. 'It's my job, Flora. I rescue people from fires.'

'I know, but you go above and beyond. You don't protect yourself enough.' She dragged in a breath. 'You could've been killed. And what would've happened to Joey, then?'

Tom stared at her. 'So what are you saying? That I should give up being a firefighter? It's who I *am*.'

'I know that.' It was like that for her, too, with her job. 'I'm not saying this right.' And she'd started to stumble over her words. 'I just don't want you to take stupid risks, Tom. It's not going to bring Ben back. It's not going to b-bring your sister back. And if you die, what about Joey?' She was shaking now, so worried and angry when she thought about what could have happened that the words spilled out before she could stop them. 'What about me?'

Tom looked utterly shocked. 'Flora, I...'

She shook her head. 'You could've been really badly hurt. If you'd been trapped under that beam, you could've been killed, or so badly burned that...' She choked the words back. 'That little girl could've died.'

'She's fine. And so am I. It's just a bit of a bruise.'

A huge bruise, she'd bet, though she couldn't make him show her. Not outside, on a chilly February night, while Joey was sitting in the car, his face white with anxiety as he looked at them.

'Joey's waiting. You'd better go.'

Tom took a step towards her, as if he was going to kiss her, and she took a step back. Not now. She was still so angry with him for taking a stupid risk, for not thinking before he acted, that she didn't want to kiss him. She wanted to shake him—shake some sense into him.

'Flora—'

'Joey's waiting,' she said again, taking another step back.

Tom's face tightened, and he got into the car without another word.

She waved as he drove off—more for Joey's sake than for Tom's—and then headed back inside.

It was the first time she could ever remember shouting at anyone. The first time she'd ever had a real fight with anyone. And it felt horrible. But what else could she have done? If Tom was taking risks like that at work…

She was miserable for the rest of the evening. When the phone rang, much later that night, she didn't answer it. The answering machine clicked in, and she heard Tom's deep voice leaving a message.

'Flora, it's me. I've been thinking about what you said, and…well, you have a point. It never occurred to me. When I'm at work, everything else is excluded. I don't think of anything except my job. And you're right, I do need to think about other things. About Joey.' He paused. 'About *you*. I'll call you tomorrow morning, OK? Bye, honey. And I'm s—'

The answering machine beeped and cut him off.

Had he just been about to apologise?

But words were easy. Actions were harder. If he wasn't prepared to put Joey first and take more care of himself, this wasn't going to work.

At practically the crack of dawn, the phone rang again. Flora answered it automatically.

'Sorry, did I wake you?' Tom asked.

'Sort of.' She hadn't slept too well.

'I apologise. But I needed to talk to you. About last night.'

'I'm sorry I shouted at you.'

'You were right,' he said softly. 'My life's different now—if

I take risks, it impacts on more than just me. I need to think about that. Properly.' He paused. 'I'm sorry for worrying you.'

'OK.' Flora had no idea what to say next. Never having had a huge row with someone, she didn't have a clue how to make up, either.

'Will you still come for dinner tonight?' he asked.

He still wanted to see her? Or—a nasty thought crept in—was it that he was worried about losing a babysitter?

'Please? And then I can apologise properly, in person.' He sighed. 'I don't want to fight with you, Flora.'

'I don't want to fight with you, either.'

'Then will you still come for dinner? Please?'

'I… OK.'

'Good. See you tonight. And I am sorry.'

'Me, too.'

She thought about it all day. What did you wear when you met your partner's parents for the first time? In the end, she decided to wear the black skirt and teal top she knew Tom liked. She left her hair loose, but put an Alice band in it to keep it off her face. She'd forgotten to ask him if she should bring red or white wine, so she played it safe and bought a decent bottle of each, plus chocolates and a magnetic fishing game for Joey. If it all went pear-shaped, she could play a game or two with Joey, then claim a headache and leave early.

Tom answered the door to her. 'Hi. You look lovely.'

'Thanks.' She felt the betraying colour seep into her face and wished she'd worn make-up, except she was hopeless at anything other than lipstick; her parents had always told her she didn't need to wear it, so she'd never joined the other girls at school in experimenting with eye-shadow and blusher. Ha. Blusher. She blushed way too much as it was.

He drew her into his arms and rested his cheek against her

hair. 'I really am sorry, honey. And you've given me a lot to think about.'

'I'm sorry, too. I was pushy.'

'You,' he said softly, 'were absolutely right.' He kissed her lightly. 'Come in.'

She handed the wine over.

'You really didn't need to bring anything,' he said, 'but thank you. That's really sweet of you.'

Joey rushed over to greet her and gave her a hug. 'For me?' he asked when she handed him the bag.

'For you,' she said with a smile.

He peeked inside. 'Oh, wow! Will you play with me, Flora?'

'If Uncle Tom says there's time before tea, of course I will. Otherwise we'll have a game afterwards,' she promised.

'Cool.' He beamed at her.

'Flora, these are my parents, Thomas and Lisa—Mum and Dad, this is Flora.' Tom introduced them swiftly.

Tom looked very like his father, Flora thought, and Thomas Nicholson was just as tall as his son; though he had hazel eyes, like Joey's. Tom had clearly inherited Lisa's eyes. 'I'm pleased to meet you both,' Flora said shyly, shaking their hands.

'I hope you like roast chicken,' Lisa said. 'It's Joey's favourite.'

'I promised you a proper home-cooked dinner tonight, so you knew I wasn't going to have anything to do with it,' Tom said with a grin, resting his hand on Flora's shoulder.

She smiled, and his parents laughed.

'Can I do anything to help?' Flora asked.

'No, love, you're fine,' Lisa said. 'Go and sit down. You've got time to play that game with Joey if you want to.'

Within five minutes, Flora had Tom and his father sitting on the floor with her and Joey, and Joey was clearly thrilled to have everyone playing with him. As well as pleasing the little boy, the game broke the ice for her, so she found it easy to answer Tom's parents' questions about herself over dinner, about her job and where she lived.

'Flora's got a farm but she used to be scared of the chickens,' Joey said. 'And she's got a way cool dog. He's called Banjo and he's a springer spaniel.'

Tom stared at his nephew, clearly dumbstruck by the fact that he was talking so much.

'She's got a picture of him on her phone,' Joey added. 'Can I show Nanna Lisa, Flora?'

'Sure.' Flora delved into her handbag, retrieved her phone and let Joey show the photo of the dog to his grandmother.

'Very cute,' Lisa said.

'He's an old softie,' Flora said with a smile.

After she'd told Joey a bedtime story and promised him another game of fishing later in the week, Flora helped Lisa wash up.

'You've been really good for Joey,' Lisa said quietly. 'And for Tom. I was so worried about the pair of them. Thomas and I were going to come back from France and help out, but Tom said it wouldn't be fair to any of us. Thomas's arthritis is bad and I'm not as young as I was; I just can't do all the things that a young lad needs people to do with him.' She sighed. 'And Joey went so quiet after the accident. He'd hardly speak; and I can see you've made a huge difference to him. You've really helped bring him back out of his shell.'

'He's a lovely boy,' Flora said, 'a real pleasure to have around.'

'And Tom—you've changed him, too,' Lisa said thoughtfully. 'He's less guarded. He doesn't use those awful jokes as a wall as much as he did.'

'He told me about Ben,' Flora said softly.

Lisa nodded. 'It changed him, when Ben died. He'd never show any emotion after that; he turned everything into a big joke and never let anyone talk to him about serious things.' She bit her lip. 'And he adored his big sister. Losing Susie hit him hard, but he just wouldn't talk about it to anyone—he clammed up or changed the subject.' She paused, looking hopeful. 'Has he talked to you about her?' Lisa looked worried sick about her son.

'He has,' Flora reassured her gently. 'It was probably easier for him to talk to me because he knew I'd been there myself—I lost both my parents last year.'

'Oh, my dear, I'm so sorry.'

'I don't have any regrets about the past,' Flora said. 'My parents knew I loved them and I knew they loved me. I would've liked a bit more time with them, but it just wasn't to be.' She shrugged. 'I miss them but, the way I see it, I'm really lucky that I had them for twenty-three years.'

Lisa hugged her. 'Tom's right, you're special.'

Tom—who, on his own mother's admission, wouldn't talk about serious things—had told his parents that she was special... There was a lump in Flora's throat as she hugged Lisa back.

She enjoyed the rest of the evening, chatting to Tom's parents over coffee and chocolates, and then realised with a shock that it was almost ten o'clock. 'I'd better get back,' she said.

'It was lovely to meet you,' Lisa said. 'And Thomas and I were thinking, you both deserve a night out, so we've booked a table for you both for tomorrow night at a little place down the road that's meant to do excellent food. It's our treat, and we've already paid the bill, so don't argue.' She smiled. 'We're going to take Joey to the pictures in St Piran's in the afternoon and have something to eat out afterwards, so you don't have to worry—we'll have a wonderful time.'

'Thank you,' Tom said, looking stunned. 'That's really nice of you, Mum.'

'I don't know what to say,' Flora said, 'except thank you. That's so kind.'

'Just enjoy it,' Lisa said, hugging them both.

CHAPTER TEN

THE meal was perfect. Beautifully cooked, beautifully presented…and Flora, for once, found it hard to eat. Because this was the first time that she and Tom had been out on a proper date, on their own. It wasn't like their fun impromptu lunches on the beach or playing in the park with Joey; this suddenly felt very serious and very grown-up. And her shyness was back to hobble her.

Then she caught Tom's eye and realised that he was as nervous as she was.

'You've gone shy on me again, and I don't have a clue why I'm so nervous,' Tom said. 'This is crazy. We talk for hours over lunch and when we're with Joey.'

'But this is different.' She swallowed hard. 'It's a proper date.'

'Our other dates were proper dates,' Tom said. 'But I know what you mean. This feels…' He paused. 'Different.'

With each course, Flora felt more and more awkward.

And then a band started playing.

'Dance with me?' Tom asked.

This was where she really ought to tell him she wasn't good at dancing. She'd never been one for the school discos, and her parents had never played the kind of music that her schoolfriends' parents had played.

'I have two left feet,' she said quietly as he led her onto

the dance floor. 'So I apologise in advance if I tread on your toes.'

'You won't,' Tom said confidently. 'My parents made Susie and I have lessons when we were teenagers. Follow my lead, and this is going to be just fine.'

To her surprise, he was right. Instead of feeling clumsy and gawky, she found herself actually dancing with him—it felt effortless, and as if she were floating. She'd never, ever experienced this before, and she loved it.

'OK?' he asked.

'Much better than OK,' she said. 'I've never been able to do this sort of thing before.'

'All you need is confidence,' Tom said softly. 'And I didn't tell you, you look lovely tonight. Your hair looks amazing.'

Flora felt as if she was glowing.

And when the music slowed down, Tom kissed her.

In public.

And although her knees had gone weak, he was holding her, supporting her, and she didn't fall flat on her face.

The evening went by way too quickly, and Flora wasn't quite ready for it to end when Tom dropped her at home.

'Would you like to come in for a coffee?' she asked.

'I'd like that. Very much.' He smiled at her.

When she switched the kettle on, he stood behind her and wrapped his arms round her waist, drawing her back against him. His mouth traced a path down the sensitive cord at the side of her neck, and she sighed with pleasure.

'Flora.'

She wriggled round in his arms and reached up to touch his cheek, rubbed her thumb along his lower lip.

Tom sighed and drew her thumb into his mouth, sucking hard; a wave of heat slid through her. When he released her thumb, he kept his hand curved round hers; he kissed the centre of her palm and folded her fingers over it, and then traced a path down to where a pulse beat rapidly in her wrist. He touched the tip of his tongue to it, and she shivered. 'Tom.'

Everything seemed to blur, and then she was in his arms, and he was kissing her properly, his mouth demanding and yet enticing at the same time, making her want more. Her arms were wrapped round his neck; his fingertips slipped under the hem of her top and he stroked her skin, the pads of his fingers moving in tiny circles.

His hands settled for a moment at the curve of her waist, then moved round to her midriff. Her heart began to beat faster as his hand moved upwards, so very slowly; she could feel her breasts tightening and her nipples hardening.

And then she panicked.

He sensed it and pulled back. 'What's wrong?'

'I…' She bit her lip, feeling a fool. How could she tell him? 'I'm not good at—at *this*,' she whispered miserably.

'Usually, when a man says that to a woman, he's the one at fault and he's trying to boost his ego at her expense,' Tom said drily. 'Just so you know, I don't think you're bad at this at all.' He stole a kiss. 'You make me feel… I don't know. I'm not good at the verbal stuff. Wonderful.' He took her hand and placed it against his chest. 'Feel that?'

His heart. Beating. Hard. Fast.

'Yes,' she whispered.

'That's what you do to me, my adorable Flora.'

She swallowed hard. He was under a real misapprehension here, and she was going to have to tell him the truth. 'Nobody actually said I was bad at it.'

'You just assumed it?' he guessed.

She shook her head. 'I…um…' Oh, why was it so hard to say?

'Tell me,' he said softly.

She felt colour shoot into her face. 'Did I just say that out loud?'

''Fraid so.' He squeezed her hand. 'What is it? Am I pushing you too fast?'

'It's not that,' she said miserably. She wanted him, all right. He made her feel the way that nobody else had ever done. 'I've always had a quiet life. I never did all the partying as a student. I was too busy studying.' Unable to face the scorn she knew she'd see in his face when he learned the truth, she closed her eyes. 'I'm still a virgin.'

Tom said nothing, and she knew she'd blown it.

'I know. It's pathetic. Twenty-four and never been touched.'

'It's not pathetic in the slightest.' To her surprise, she found herself lifted off her feet and carried over to the sofa. Tom sat down and settled her on his lap. 'You're not pathetic at all,' he said fiercely. 'You're a lot of things, but you're definitely not pathetic.' He traced her lower lip with the pad of his thumb. 'You're beautiful. You're sweet. You make me feel as if I could conquer the world.'

'But?' She could see it in his eyes. A huge, enormous, horrible *but*.

'But,' he said, 'I want to behave honourably towards you.' He grimaced. 'Actually, no, I don't. I want to carry you upstairs and kiss you and touch you until you feel as if you're dissolving. I want to make you feel as amazing as you make me feel.'

She swallowed hard. 'But my virginity's in the way.'

'It's something precious,' he said. 'Not something you should throw away. You should hold out for the right person.'

'So I'll be a virgin on my wedding night? That's…' She shook her head. 'That's so old-fashioned, Tom. I'm twenty-four years old and this is the twenty-first century.' She bit her lip.

'When I was at school, all the cool girls used to laugh at me. Fat, frumpy Flora, they called me. They always said I was so old-fashioned. And I hated it, Tom. I wanted to be cool, just like them.'

'No.' He wrapped his arms round her, pulling her closer. 'You're better than cool. You're real. Genuine. And, just for the record, you're not fat. You're deliciously curvy. And you're not frumpy—you're natural, rather than being caked in gunk.'

'But you're going to leave and go home now. And you're not going to touch me again.' And the knowledge made her feel as if her heart had cracked right down the middle.

'Because I'm trying very hard to do the right thing,' Tom said. 'To be honourable.'

'What if,' she said slowly, 'I don't want you to be honourable?'

His eyes darkened. 'What are you saying?'

'What if…?' she said. 'What if I want to go to bed with you? It's not as if I don't know the theory—I'm a nurse. I just…haven't done the practical side of things before, that's all.'

Colour slashed along his cheekbones. 'Are you sure about this, Flora?'

She was as nervous as hell, and her voice was shaking, but she said the words and meant them. 'I'm sure.'

'Absolutely sure?' he checked.

In answer, she kissed him. Hard.

'No pressure,' he said softly, and kissed her again. 'My beautiful, adorable Flora. Do you have any idea how precious the gift you're giving me is?'

'I want you, Tom,' she whispered.

'I'm with you all the way, honey,' he said, his voice husky. He scooped her up in his arms again and carried her up the stairs.

'What about your back? You were hurt on Friday.'

'I'm fine. Nothing that a hot bath couldn't sort out. And, right now, all I can think of is how much I want to make love with you.' He kissed her, his mouth hot and arousing. 'Which one's your bedroom?'

'On the left.'

He opened the door, then gradually let her down until her feet were touching the floor, keeping her body pressed close to his all the way so that she was left in no doubt of his arousal.

Doubts flickered through her again. A man as gorgeous as Tom had no doubt dated plenty of girls. Girls who knew what they were doing.

'What's the matter?' he asked softly.

'Just…I don't want to disappoint you.'

He switched on the bedside light, then got her to sit down on the edge of the bed and knelt down in front of her. He took both her hands in his. 'Look me in the eye, Flora Loveday.'

She did so.

'Now listen to what I'm telling you. You're not going to disappoint me. *Ever*,' he emphasised. 'And I'm going to do my best to make sure this is good for you. If I do anything that makes you feel uncomfortable, just tell me and I'll stop.' He drew her hands to his mouth. 'You have no idea how much self-control I'm having to use, right now. But I'm going to take this slowly, because I want to enjoy every single second of this. And I want you to enjoy it even more.'

Excitement rippled through her.

'Flora,' he said, his voice low and sensual, 'I'd like to see you.'

She felt incredibly self-conscious, but lifted her arms and let him peel her top up and over her head.

Then she remembered that she was wearing a very plain, functional bra. How she wished she'd bought something frivolous and lacy. She crossed her hands automatically over her breasts, not wanting him to see the boring, frumpy garment.

'You want me to stop?' he asked.

She bit her lip and shook her head. 'It's not that.'

'What, then?' His voice was very, very gentle.

'My bra's horrible. It's embarrassing.'

He smiled at her. 'I have an idea. Let's get it out of the way, so it doesn't spoil this for you. How about I close my eyes and undo your bra without looking?' His smile went all the way up into his eyes and she knew that he was laughing with her, not at her.

'I'm being silly, aren't I?'

'No, you're not—and I want the first time to be good for you,' he said. 'You're beautiful.' He kissed her lightly. 'And now I'm closing my eyes.' He deftly removed her bra and dropped it on the floor.

And then he opened his eyes and sucked in a breath. 'Wow. *Flora*. I don't know what I want to do first—touch you or taste you or just look at you. You're *gorgeous*.'

The expression on his face told her that he was completely sincere; Flora blushed again, but this time from pleasure rather than embarrassment.

He was still kneeling in front of her; he cupped her breasts in his hands, lifting them up and together and teasing her nipples with the pads of his thumbs. 'Seriously, seriously gorgeous. And your skin's so soft.' He swallowed hard. 'Flora, I really need to…'

'Yes,' she whispered, and he dipped his head, closing his mouth round one nipple.

She knew the theory.

But she hadn't been prepared at all for the way Tom made her feel. The surge of desire that ran through her entire body; the hot, wet, tight feeling between her thighs; the need for *more*. More of what, exactly, she wasn't sure, but she needed it. She slid her hands into his hair and drew him closer.

He paid attention to her other nipple, and she arched against him. 'Tom,' she whispered.

He stopped and looked up at her; and she noticed just how wide his pupils were. Huge with desire. 'Yes, honey?'

'I want to see you, too.'

He smiled. 'OK.' He removed his tie and dropped it on the floor, then undid the top button of his shirt and spread his arms. 'I'm in your hands. Do what you want with me.'

All hers.

Wow.

She unbuttoned his shirt, revealing strong pectoral muscles and a sprinkling of hair on his chest. 'You're beautiful, Tom.'

She slid the soft cotton from his shoulders and enjoyed stroking his bare skin, feeling his musculature tightening under her touch.

'My turn now?' he asked. At her nod, he said, 'Stand up.' He unzipped her skirt and let it slide to the floor; her slip went the same way, and then he slowly peeled her tights down, stroking her skin as he moved lower. 'Gorgeous. And all mine,' he said, pressing a kiss against her navel.

Flora sucked in her stomach, feeling self-conscious, and he stood up, too.

'We need to even this up a bit.'

She knew what he meant. Her hands were shaking as she undid the button of his trousers and then lowered his zip; she eased the material down over his hips and he stepped out of his trousers, heeling off his shoes and his socks as he did so. His underpants outlined his arousal, and he was bigger than she'd expected. Help. This was going to be the very first time; she wasn't sure whether she felt more nervous or excited.

Maybe it showed in her face, she thought, when Tom said

softly, 'Let me tell you how this is going to be. I'm going to touch you, and kiss you, all over. You can do whatever you like to me. And then...' his breath hitched '...then I'm going to make you completely mine.'

Gently, he lifted her up and laid her against the pillows, then climbed onto the bed beside her. He kissed and stroked his way down her body, clearly taking notice of what made her react more strongly because he lingered in some places and skated over others. He took his time exploring her with his mouth and hands, from the hollows of her collarbones down to the soft undersides of her breasts, her navel, her hipbones.

And then, just when she thought he was going to cup her sex with his hand and deal with the ache inside her, he shifted and started from her feet, stroking her insteps and kissing the hollows of her ankles. She discovered that the backs of her knees was definitely an erogenous zone; her sex felt hot and wet and tight, and it was as if her body was slowly being wound up to a pitch.

Finally, he slid his fingertips under the waistband of her knickers and drew the material down.

'You're so beautiful,' he whispered, 'absolutely gorgeous— and I need to touch you, Flora. I really, really need to touch you.'

'Yes.' She barely recognised her voice, it was so low and husky.

He kept his eyes locked with hers as he stroked her inner thigh. Anticipation made her breath hitch; she had no idea how this was going to be, how it was going to make her feel.

And then, at last, he let one finger glide across her sex, and she found out.

Like nothing on earth.

A shiver of pure desire went through her. 'Oh, Tom,' she whispered.

He wasn't going to...?

Her cheeks flamed as he knelt between her thighs.

And then she stopped thinking at all as his tongue flicked lightly over her clitoris. She slid her hands into his hair, sighing his name—not really knowing what she was asking for, but knowing that he was driving her crazy.

He teased her with his mouth and his fingers. Her body tensed even further, to the point where she didn't think she was going to be able to handle any more, and then suddenly the pressure peaked and released, shocking her with the depths of pleasure. She cried out his name.

He shifted up to hold her close. 'OK?'

'I think so.' She felt the colour in her face deepen. 'I didn't realise it would be like that. It was incredible, Tom.'

He stroked her face. 'Do you know how it makes me feel, knowing I'm the first person who's been able to make you feel like this? As if I'm king of the world,' he said softly.

'I feel pretty good myself,' she said, her voice shaking.

'This is just the start, honey,' he promised.

She wasn't sure when he'd removed his underpants, but when he climbed off the bed she was left in no doubt of just how big and how strong Tom Nicholson was. Though she knew he'd be gentle with her; he'd already given her pleasure she'd never dreamed existed, and he was planning more.

He found his wallet in his pocket and removed a condom.

'OK?' he asked. 'If you want to wait, that's fine.'

'No—I want you, Tom.' I want you to love me, she thought—and realised in that moment that she loved him, absolutely. It didn't matter that she hadn't known him that long; he was kind, gorgeous and strong, and she trusted him to keep her safe.

He rolled the condom on and knelt between her thighs, nudging them apart, then bent to kiss her. 'You're beautiful,

Flora. You take my breath away. And I've wanted this almost since the first moment I met you.'

A thrill went through her at his words. 'You're beautiful, too.'

Slowly, slowly, he eased into her. She felt a sharp twinge and he must've realised it too, because he paused, giving her time to get used to his weight and the feel of him.

'OK, honey?' he asked.

She nodded. 'Very OK.'

'You're sure I'm not hurting you?'

'Not any more.'

He kissed her, then lifted her hips so he could push deeper into her. And then Flora discovered that he'd been telling the truth, that the first climax was just the start. Pleasure started to build and build again; warmth spread through her, coiling and pulling tight, and then the release hit her.

She felt his body tighten inside hers; she looked into his eyes and saw them go wide with pleasure as his own climax hit.

He held her tightly afterwards. 'My adorable Flora,' he said softly.

Finally, he gently withdrew from her. 'I'll be back in a moment, honey.' He was completely unselfconscious as he left the bed, but Flora wriggled in embarrassment. She couldn't just lie there, naked, waiting for him to come back. Should she get dressed, or would he expect her to stay in bed? Unsure, and feeling ridiculously shy, she grabbed the duvet to cover herself.

When Tom came back, he was smiling. 'You, Flora Loveday, are a wonderful woman, and I feel incredibly privileged.'

He climbed into bed beside her and pulled her into his arms. 'Right now, I just want to hold you; it feels wonderful to have you in my arms, your skin against mine.' He brushed a kiss over her temples. 'What I'd really like to do is fall asleep with you in my arms and wake up with you in the morning, but I can't do that—it's not fair to Mum and Dad.'

'What's the time?' She glanced at her bedside clock. 'They'll already be worried about you.'

'It's almost midnight. They won't be expecting me back just yet—they knew when they booked the table that there was a band as well, and they'll guess that I'll have coffee with you.'

She bit her lip. 'I didn't actually make you any coffee.'

He smiled. 'You can remedy that some other time. I'm not going anywhere and you sure as hell aren't moving from my arms right now.'

Gradually her tension eased, and it felt good to lie in his arms like this, with her head against his shoulder. Little by little, her eyes closed, and Flora finally fell asleep, warm and comfortable.

CHAPTER ELEVEN

Tom wished he could stay in bed beside Flora all night—but he couldn't. His carefree bachelor life was gone now; and, even though he knew that his nephew would be perfectly safe with his grandparents, he also knew that it wouldn't be fair to them if he stayed here with Flora. They'd worry that something had happened to him, and the car crash that had taken Susie and Kevin from them would be uppermost in their minds. He couldn't put them through that kind of torment. And it wouldn't be fair to Joey, either; the little boy needed security, and seeing Tom there in the morning would help.

Reluctantly, and careful not to wake Flora as he did so, Tom wriggled out of the bed and dressed swiftly. She looked so peaceful that he couldn't bear to wake her. But he also wasn't just going to walk out and abandon her. Not when she'd given him something so very precious.

He tiptoed downstairs, and Banjo was instantly alert.

'Shh, she's asleep. Don't bark,' Tom said softly.

He went over to the memo pad by her phone and scribbled a quick note.

You look adorable, asleep—couldn't bring myself to wake you! Have to get back to Joey, but will call you in the morning. T x

He left the note propped against the kettle, where she'd be bound to find it in the morning, made a brief fuss of Banjo and persuaded the dog back to his basket, then quietly let himself out of the house.

Driving back to his flat, he thought about Flora. The way she'd responded to him. The wonder in her eyes.

And then it hit him.

He'd felt that exact same sense of wonder. And not just because he'd known that this was a big deal for her—it had been a big deal for him, too. He'd never really let himself connect with anyone in the past: but tonight he'd connected with Flora. Heart and soul. It was like nothing he'd ever experienced before.

Oh, hell.

He'd always promised himself that he'd never let his relationships get serious. It wasn't fair to expect someone else to face the burden of the risks he took every day in his job.

And yet he'd done it. Fallen for her completely. Her warmth, her kindness, the sweetness in her smile—everything about her drew him. And, at some point over the last couple of weeks, he'd stopped guarding his heart. More than that, he'd actually given his heart to her. Freely and completely.

Oh, double hell.

What did he do now?

Because now the whole world was different. Two months ago, he'd been a carefree bachelor, enjoying life as a single man. Now he was a stand-in father to someone who'd lost almost his whole world—and he couldn't risk letting Joey lose the bits he had left. And he wasn't a carefree bachelor any more: he was involved with Flora. Really involved with her, from the centre of his heart.

Letting Joey down wasn't an option.

Un-falling in love with Flora also wasn't an option; being with her had shown him that, before, he'd only been living part of a life. There was much more to it than working hard, and playing just as hard. Football was fun, but teaching Joey how to dribble and score goals was even better. And as for parties with loud music…maybe he'd suddenly grown up overnight, but he discovered that he'd rather have a walk on the beach and a soundtrack of laughter.

With Flora and Joey, he could have a real family. The same kind of love his parents had. The same kind of happiness his sister had had.

But Flora had made him think, the other night, and now he knew that the happiness and love were bitter-sweet: at any time a fire could turn rogue and take him from them. He'd be forced to let them down in the most fundamental way, unable to fight his way back to them.

On paper, it was easy. All he had to do was take the danger out of his life so they wouldn't have to shoulder the risk of losing him.

Change his job.

In real life it wasn't quite as simple as that. As he'd told her the other night, fighting fires and rescuing people wasn't just his job, it was who he *was*. He'd joined the fire brigade at eighteen, straight after his A levels, and had never looked back. How could he walk away from the job he loved, from what'd he'd done for almost half his life and the whole of his adult life?

Without that, he didn't have a clue what he'd do.

But maybe the small hours of the morning wasn't the best time to make decisions. He needed to sit down and work out what all his options were. Make a rational decision. Do the right thing.

When he let himself quietly into the flat, he discovered that his mother was waiting up for him. 'Did you have a nice time?'

'Wonderful, thanks,' he said as he sat next to her on the sofa.

'Sure? You look a bit worried,' Lisa said.

'I'm fine. I just realised I'm a bit late back,' he fibbed, 'and I didn't want you to be worrying about me.'

'It doesn't matter that you're six feet four and thirty-two years old. You're still my baby and always will be, so I'll always worry about you,' Lisa said with a smile, ruffling his hair.

'Is Joey all right?'

'Yes, and we all ate far too much ice cream, was lovely—just like taking you and Susie to the cinema when you were little.'

'Mmm, I remember.' He gave her a wistful smile. 'I had a really happy childhood, Mum.'

'Good. That's what we wanted.'

'That's what I want for Joey, too.' He sighed. 'And I'm not making a very good job of it. Flora's helped a huge amount, but…I'm never going to be good enough, Mum.'

'Don't do yourself down, love. Joey's been through a lot. But he knows you're there for him and he knows you love him, and that's going to help him through,' Lisa said. 'Don't worry. It's all going to be fine. You're doing your best, and that's all anyone can ask.' She kissed the top of his head. 'I'd better let you get some sleep. See you in the morning.'

Tom lay awake for much of the night, trying to work out what he ought to do. But he still hadn't come to a decent compromise the next morning. He showered, dressed and made himself a mug of tea, then Joey appeared.

'I hear you ate lots of ice cream yesterday,' Tom said as he poured his nephew a glass of milk.

Joey nodded.

'How was the film?'

'Good. Can we play fishing?'

Tom smiled. 'Sure we can.'

They were in the middle of their third game when his mother emerged from the bedroom, wrapped in a towelling robe and yawning.'

'The kettle's hot, Mum. Do you want some tea?' Tom asked.

'Thank you, darling.'

When Joey went to get dressed, Tom asked quietly, 'Mum, would you mind very much if I sneaked over and had breakfast with Flora this morning?'

Lisa raised an eyebrow. 'She's really important to you, isn't she?'

He smiled. 'I'm not answering that one.'

'Well, she's the first girl you've actually let us meet—and that tells me a lot. She's lovely,' Lisa said. 'I like her very much, and I think she'll make you happy.'

'Mmm, but it's whether I'll be able to make her happy.' He bit his lip. 'I'm a firefighter.'

'And she's a nurse, so she's going to understand the demands of your job a lot more than someone who doesn't work in the emergency services.'

'Maybe.'

'Are you thinking about giving it up, love?'

'I don't know.' He sighed. 'Mum, being a firefighter. It's who I am. I can't see myself as anything else—the world wouldn't feel right. But…I've got Joey to think of now, and Flora, and… It's a lot for them to have to put up with. All that worry.' He shook his head. 'I can't work this out.'

'And I'm not the person you should be talking it over with,' Lisa said softly. 'Find out what Flora thinks.'

He already knew what she thought. That his job was dangerous and he took reckless risks that could mean Joey was left alone.

'Talk it over with her. But don't rush into anything.'

He smiled wryly. 'Yes, you're right. It's too fast. I've only known her for a few days.'

'That's not what I meant—when you meet the right one, you'll know.' Lisa smiled. 'And I think you might just have met your "the one", in Flora. I've never seen you like this about anyone else. No, I meant you need to talk things through and weigh up all your options, not just rush in and do what you think is the right thing. Now go and have breakfast with your girl. We'll see you later.'

'Where are you going?' Joey asked when he came back from his room, fully dressed and wearing odd socks.

'To see Flora,' Tom told him.

'Can I come?'

'Another time,' Lisa said, 'because I want you to teach me how to make that lovely French toast you say Flora makes. How about being Chef Joey and taking Grandpa some breakfast in bed?'

Tom gave his mother a grateful look, and kissed both her and Joey goodbye. 'I'll be back soon. Flora has to be at work at half past eight.'

He called in at the out-of-town supermarket on the way to the farm and bought flowers and croissants. When he rang the doorbell, Flora took a while to answer, and she was wearing her dressing gown, so he'd clearly woken her.

'Perfect timing,' he said with a grin. 'This means I can have breakfast with you and then I can have a shower with you.'

'Tom Nicholson, that's shocking!' But she was smiling. 'I wasn't expecting to see you this morning.'

'Mum and Dad are with Joey and I wanted to see you for breakfast.' He handed her the flowers. 'These, because you're beautiful.'

She sniffed them. 'Thank you, they're lovely.'

'And these, because… Oh, wait. Forget about the healthy

eating stuff you do with your classes. These, because they're the nicest breakfast ever.'

She peered into the bag and laughed. 'I love croissants, too. And I have posh strawberry jam from the farm shop.'

'Brilliant.' He paused. 'Did you find my note this morning?'

She smiled. 'Yes. I have to admit, I felt a bit strange when I woke up and you weren't there, but I knew you had to get back for Joey.'

'I wish I'd woken with you.' He stroked her face. 'You look so cute when you're asleep. Like a little dormouse.'

'A dormouse?' She raised an eyebrow. 'Thanks. I think.' But her eyes were sparkling.

She made them both coffee, put the flowers in water, and Tom thoroughly enjoyed feeding her croissants and licking jam from her fingers. Not to mention having a shower with her after breakfast.

'Tom, I'm going to be late!' she said, sounding shocked, when they finally made it back to her bedroom and she glanced at her clock.

'No, you won't. I'll drop you at the surgery. Do you need your car this afternoon?'

'Only to get home.'

'That's easy, then. I'll pick you up,' Tom said. 'I thought maybe we could take Joey out ten-pin bowling and then eat out at that new burger place.'

'That'd be lovely. Provided you let it be my treat,' she added. 'And I insist on that.'

Flora made it to the surgery with three minutes to spare. Kate Tremayne smiled at Flora as she walked in. 'I'm not going to ask,' Kate said, 'but it's lovely to see you sparkling like this.'

Was what she'd just done with Tom so obvious? Flora felt herself blush to the roots of her hair. 'Um…'

Kate laughed. 'It couldn't happen to a nicer couple. And Tom's a sweetie.'

Flora was gobsmacked. 'How did you know?'

Kate raised an eyebrow. 'Penhally's not exactly a huge place—and when you're holding hands on the beach with someone, you can expect someone to spot you.' She paused. 'And Nick took me out to dinner last night. The food's good at The Mackerel, isn't it?'

'You were there?' Flora looked at her, aghast. 'I'm so sorry I was rude and didn't say anything to you. I just didn't see you.'

Kate smiled. 'I know, love. You two only had eyes for each other.'

Flora felt her blush deepen. 'I guess so.'

She discovered during her surgery that morning, while doing a blood-pressure check for one of her patients, that Kate hadn't been the only person to see her and Tom at the restaurant.

Worse still, Mrs Evans, whose venous ulcer she was dressing, had seen Tom kissing her goodbye in the surgery car park that morning.

'Your young man's a lovely boy. He rescued my neighbour's dog from the river last week, and he never made a fuss when Goldie bit him—he's a smashing young lad,' Mrs Evans said. 'He's a keeper, you mark my words.'

By lunchtime, Flora realised that quite a few people in Penhally had already got her and Tom married off, and her protests that it was still very early days were just ignored.

'You make a lovely couple, dear,' was the standard response.

She just hoped that Tom wasn't getting the same kind of comments, or he might start avoiding her.

But he was there with Joey to meet her from work, and Joey greeted her with a hug. They made a quick stop back at the farmhouse to let Banjo out and feed him, then went off ten-pin bowling. Tom put the bumper bars up on their lane and got Joey to use the ramp, and Joey was thrilled to get a strike.

This, Flora thought, was what it felt like to be a family.

And she loved it.

Josh scanned the hospital canteen as he walked in: force of habit. Most of the time, Megan wasn't there. It was as if she had some kind of radar system that told her when he was having a break so she could avoid him.

But then he saw her at a table in a quiet corner. On her own.

It was too good a chance to miss. He headed straight over to her table. 'Megan.'

Her eyes widened. 'I'm about to go.'

'Don't go,' he said softly. 'Stay and talk to me. I'm just going to get myself a sandwich. Can I get you a coffee?'

'I…'

She was wavering; hope bloomed within him. 'I saw you at the football match, the other week.' And she'd avoided him at the hospital ever since.

'I was just passing.'

That might've been true, because the football pitch was halfway between St Piran's and Penhally, where Megan lived. But she wouldn't be 'just passing' after her shift at that time of the morning. Not that he was going to call her on it. He didn't want her to bolt. 'Stay and have coffee with me?'

Hell, she was beautiful. Even with her hair pulled back for work, she was beautiful. And he knew exactly what her hair looked like when it was tumbled over her shoulders. Tumbled over his pillow. Soft and silky and…

He dragged in a breath. Not now. He needed to take this slowly. Get her to talk to him again. 'Please, Megan?'

She looked wary, but she nodded. 'OK.'

Josh wanted to punch the air. 'Back in a second, OK?'

Even though he grabbed the first sandwich he could see from the chiller, by the time he'd paid for them and two coffees, he could see that Megan had changed her mind.

'Sorry. My bleep just went.'

She might've been using it as an excuse; then again, it might not be. Her department was busy.

But this felt just a little too convenient.

'Sorry,' she said again, and fled.

Tom and Joey met Flora at the surgery on Tuesday with a picnic basket; although it was cold, it was dry and for once not windy. They ate sandwiches on the beach, then went for a walk to collect shells.

'So have you thought any more about going to the football dinner with me?' Tom asked.

'I'm still thinking about it,' she admitted.

'Sure. I don't want to rush you.'

Which made her feel even worse, because he was being so patient with her. The dinner was less than a week away, and there would be a cut-off point for getting tickets.

But she still couldn't help thinking that someone as popular as Tom could have absolutely anyone he wanted. Was he only spending time with her for Joey's sake? And besides, despite what they'd shared on Sunday night, he hadn't actually said he loved her—just that she made him feel amazing.

Was she expecting too much? All she'd ever wanted was someone who loved her for herself. Could Tom be that man?

And why couldn't she shake the feeling that this was all going to go horribly wrong?

Flora was miserable all evening; and, at the surgery the next morning, Kate Tremayne came in to the treatment room and closed the door behind her.

'Are you OK, Flora?'

Flora summoned a smile. 'Of course I am,' she lied.

'Don't fib.' Kate put her hands on her hips. 'You've got five minutes before your first patient. Now talk.'

Flora opened her mouth to say that nothing was wrong—but ended up spilling all her doubts. She finished miserably, 'He's asked me to go to the football league dinner with him, and I don't have a clue what to wear—I don't exactly go to posh dinners. And, if I do go, he's going to be surrounded with people all night and I won't know anyone there.'

Kate squeezed her hand. 'Love, first of all, Tom sees you exactly as you are—and you're lovely. You probably will know people there, because there are a few medics who play in the league. So I think you should say yes. Go to St Piran on Saturday morning, buy yourself a fabulous dress, and knock his socks off.'

Flora was none too sure that she'd be able to do that, but she knew that Kate meant well. 'Thanks, Kate. I will,' she said.

On Thursday, Flora went to the science museum with Tom and Joey. Not having children of her own, she'd never visited it before, and she loved it as much as Joey did.

Tom and Joey insisted on trying every single one of the interactive exhibits—from Joey standing inside a giant bubble, through to doing a duet on the giant keyboard where you pressed the notes with your feet, and making a tornado inside a bottle. The bubble show—where the woman on stage actually managed to set bubbles on fire—and the planetarium shows were also a huge hit with Joey. And Flora discovered a whole heap of leaflets they could take home to make their own experiments. 'We're definitely going to have to try making our own slime—what colour d'you reckon, Joey?'

'Green,' Joey said enthusiastically.

She laughed. 'Good call.'

She took photographs of Tom and his nephew together, having fun.

'Excuse me, love.' A middle-aged woman smiled at her. 'Would you like me to take a picture of the three of you? I know how it is when you're always the one behind the camera.'

The three of them.

Like a family.

'That'd be wonderful,' Flora said warmly, and returned the compliment by taking a picture of the woman with her grandchildren.

Tom had reverted completely to being a child, and Flora found his enthusiasm adorable. Over lunch, he looked through Flora's leaflets.

'Making a plastic out of milk? Oh, now, we have to do that. Hey, Joey, did you know this is how they used to make windows for aeroplanes in the Second World War?'

'Really?' Joey asked, wide-eyed.

'That's what it says here.'

'Wow.' Then Joey smiled. 'This is the best day ever.'

Flora, seeing the look of relief mingled with delight on Tom's face, had a lump in her throat.

Tom hugged his nephew, and then Flora. 'I'm having a brilliant day here, too, and I wouldn't have wanted to share this with anyone else except you two.'

'Snap,' Flora said. 'I never knew this sort of place could be so much fun.'

'It's just the best,' Joey said.

* * *

That evening, when Joey was in bed, Tom said, 'So what do you want to do on Saturday?'

She frowned. 'I thought you were going to the football dinner?'

'Not without you,' he said. 'And you've been avoiding the subject, so I know you don't really want to go.'

She sighed. 'Tom, they're your friends and it's something you all look forward to at the end of the season, isn't it?'

'Absolutely,' he agreed, 'but if it's the choice of going to the dinner or spending time with you, it's a no-brainer.'

He'd really give up something he was looking forward to, for her? She remembered what Kate had said. *Tom sees you exactly as you are...I think you should say yes.*

She stroked his face. 'Tom, I'm not going to stop you going.'

'I don't want to go without you. Come with me, honey.' He stole a kiss. 'I know you're probably worrying that you won't know anyone there, but they're a nice bunch and they won't shut you out.'

They had at the football match, Flora thought.

Although she didn't say it aloud, her reservations must have shown on her face because Tom said softly, 'You'll be part of the crowd because you're with me—you're my girl.'

And this time he'd be with her instead of running around on a pitch, so it might be different. She took a deep breath. It was time to be brave about this. 'What's the dress code?'

'Black tie.'

Which meant a cocktail dress—and she didn't possess one. 'I'd better go shopping, then.'

'You'll really come with me?'

She nodded.

He hugged her. 'I'm so glad. I'll go shopping with you, if you like.'

'No. Joey would hate being dragged round dress shops.' She

smiled. 'And anyway, I'd like to surprise you.' She thought again about what Kate said. *Knock his socks off.* Maybe, just maybe, it was time to stop being shy, frumpy Flora and show Tom that she was a woman who was worthy of him.

CHAPTER TWELVE

ON SATURDAY afternoon, Flora drove to St Piran. She couldn't see any dresses that would suit her in the first three shops she went into, and the assistants in the fourth turned out to be really snooty; she didn't even approach them, because she could see them mentally sizing her and wondering what on earth she thought she was doing in their shop when they were so clearly in the market for people five dress sizes smaller.

But then she saw a beautiful floaty dress in the window of a little boutique. It probably wasn't right for her, but maybe there was something else that would catch her eye.

'Can I help you?' the assistant asked.

'I'm just looking,' Flora said.

'For anything special?'

The assistant looked genuinely interested and didn't give the impression that she would only be interested in selling size-eight clothes. 'I'm going to a black-tie dinner. I need a cocktail dress, and I don't have a clue what will suit me.'

The assistant's eyes lit up. 'Would you trust me to pick something for you?'

'I... Well, sure.'

To her surprise, the assistant didn't even ask her size. She looked through the racks and picked out several dresses in very bright colours—the kind of colours that Flora never wore.

'Should I have a black dress?' Flora asked.

The assistant smiled. 'Your colouring's gorgeous, so don't hide yourself in black.'

Help, Flora thought. I don't want to stand out from the crowd.

The assistant put a gentle hand on her shoulder. 'Is he special?'

'Yes.'

'Then you'll stand out from the crowd for him anyway, so you might as well do it properly.'

Flora was beginning to agree until the assistant handed her a bright turquoise dress. It had a wrap front with a V-neck and wide shoulder straps, plus layers of silk georgette in the skirt, and it was much shorter than the kind of thing she normally wore, finishing just at the knee. She looked dubiously at it. 'I don't think I'm thin enough to wear this.'

'This shape will look fantastic on you. Just try it on and see what you think,' the assistant coaxed. 'If you hate it we'll try something else.'

Flora looked at a dress with a much higher neck. 'Something like that.'

'That's absolutely wrong for you—you need to be tall and a stick insect to suit that style,' the assistant said. 'You're much better off with something that flatters you, like this, or maybe an Empire-line dress.'

Flora knew when she was beaten and tried the dress on. To her surprise, it looked amazing.

'Just what I thought. Hang on, you need accessories.' A couple of moments later, the assistant returned with a turquoise and silver pendant, and a pair of silver strappy shoes with medium kitten heels. 'Try these. And if you wear your hair up with just a couple of curls tumbling down to soften your face…' She demonstrated, and Flora stared at herself in the mirror, barely recognising herself.

'And you're so lucky—you have fabulous skin. All you need

is a touch of eyeliner, mascara and lipstick—you're going to look amazing, and he's going to think he's the luckiest man on earth,' the assistant finished with a smile.

'Thank you—you've been really kind.'

The assistant smiled. 'My pleasure. It's lovely to be asked for advice instead of having someone come in with set ideas who refuses to try something that'd really suit them.' She paused. 'Forgive me for being rude, but you know the other way of giving yourself loads of confidence?'

'No.' Flora knew she needed all the help she could get on that front.

'Really, *really* nice underwear.'

Flora loved the silk and lace confections that the assistant showed her, and couldn't resist a buying matching set. The whole outfit came to quite a bit more than she'd intended to pay, but she didn't care. In this underwear and this dress, she was going to feel fantastic—and she was going to knock Tom's socks off.

On impulse, she texted Kate when she got home. *'Thanks for your advice. Found really lovely dress.'*

Two minutes later, her phone rang. 'That's great. What about your hair and make-up?' Kate asked.

'The shop assistant said I should wear my hair up. I was going to see if Maureen could fit me in this afternoon at the salon.'

'On a Saturday afternoon in half-term, you'll be lucky.' Kate paused. 'Let me come over and do your hair and make-up, then I can see the dress as well.'

'Kate, I can't ask you to do that.'

'You're not asking, I'm telling you,' Kate retorted.

It was the work of only a few minutes. When Flora looked in the mirror, she could hardly believe it was her. Kate hadn't caked her with make-up, and yet her eyes looked huge and luminous, and her mouth was a perfect rosebud.

'You're going to have an amazing time.' Kate hugged her. 'Let yourself be happy with Tom, Flora. You deserve each other.'

Tom arrived at seven to pick her up. When she opened the door, he didn't say a word, and Flora's heart plummeted. She'd thought she looked good. Had she got it so wrong? And then Tom blew out a breath. 'Flora. You— I— You…' He shook his head. 'I'm gibbering. Sorry. You look so fantastic, I can't remember how to speak. That dress… God, I want to carry you upstairs to bed right now and forget about the dinner dance.'

Flora was lost for words.

'But I'm not going to,' Tom continued, 'because I want to show you off.' He smiled at her. 'You always look lovely to me, but tonight…tonight, you're *glowing*.'

Confidence, she thought. Confidence that Tom had given her.

When they arrived at the dance, as Flora expected, Tom was in demand; but he kept his arm round her the whole time and introduced her to everyone on his table. A couple of them knew her anyway from the village, but to her pleasure everyone seemed to accept her.

'Weren't you at the football match, the other week?' one of them asked.

Flora bit her lip. 'Um, yes.'

'I didn't realise you were with Tom or I'd have asked you to come over and join us,' she said. 'You must've thought we were all so snooty.'

'I did feel a bit out of place,' Flora admitted.

'I'm so sorry. Tom never brings his girlfriends to anything, so I just assumed you were with another crowd. Well, I'm Cindy, and it's lovely to meet you.' She beamed at Flora. 'And it's especially lovely seeing our Tom so happy.'

Over the next few minutes, Flora discovered that, actually,

she *was* a part of Tom's crowd. She was included in the general teasing about how the wives forced the men to hold the league dinner to make up for all those weekend afternoons spent freezing on the sidelines of a football pitch and the amount of scrubbing they had to do to get the mud out of their kit. She discovered that people were interested in what she did, and interested in her opinion. It wasn't just the champagne that made her feel heady: it was Tom, because he made sure that he was sitting next to her with his arm round her shoulders, more or less telling the whole world that she was his.

Megan was really beginning to regret accepting the invitation to the football league dinner. If she'd known that Josh would be there, she wouldn't have come.

Oh, who was she kidding? Seeing him was torture—and yet not seeing him was just as bad.

This whole thing was a mess. No way was she a home wrecker, the sort of woman who destroyed someone else's marriage on a whim. Her feelings for Josh—despite the fact she'd tried to bury them for all those years—were still the same. But she knew it wasn't going to lead anywhere. How could it? Too much had happened.

And there was Rebecca.

Beautiful, fragile Rebecca.

No, she couldn't be the one to destroy Josh's marriage. To hurt another woman the way that she'd been hurt.

When Tom was dancing with Flora, a tall, glamorous, slinky blonde came up to them. 'Tom. Make sure you save a dance for me, yes?'

Tom simply smiled. 'Sorry. Tonight I'm dancing with my girl, and only my girl—and anyone who wants to dance with her is just going to be disappointed, too.'

'Tom, I'm not that insecure,' Flora said. Not any more. 'If you want to dance with your friends, that's fine.'

'That's the point.' Tom stole a kiss and drew her closer. 'There's only one person I want to dance with tonight. She's in my arms, right now—and that's how it's staying.'

'Dance with me?'

No. Tell him no. Tell him you don't dance.

And yet Megan found herself on the dance floor with Josh.

And he *would* choose to show off with a waltz. Typical Josh.

'I've missed you,' he said. 'You've been avoiding me.'

'You know why.'

'How would I know, when you never talk to me, Megan?'

A muscle flickered in her jaw. 'There's nothing to talk about, Josh.'

Josh's eyes became pleading. 'Megan.'

'You have a wife,' she said crisply, taking a step back that forced him to drop his hands from the dance hold. 'Maybe you should be talking to her. Go home, Josh.' And, just to make sure that he couldn't follow her, she headed for the ladies' toilets.

Josh stared after her. Hell, he hadn't meant to upset her. He just wanted to… No, he wanted *her*. And he realised yet again what a huge mistake he'd made, all those years back. He should never have married Rebecca; he'd tried to anaesthetise his feelings and in the end he'd been unfair to all of them. Himself included.

So what now? He and Rebecca didn't want the same things any more. They'd agreed before they'd married that there would be no children; and now Rebecca had changed her mind, was desperate for a baby; but Josh knew that having a baby wouldn't repair their broken marriage. If anything, their marriage would crack even further under the strain. And Josh had lived in a family fractured by the pressure of children. He'd been forced to take the place of his excuse of a father— of course he couldn't have stood by and watched his mother struggle on her own—and no way did he want to go back to that. One generation of that was enough.

Frustrated, hurt and completely confused, Josh headed for the bar.

'Are you all right?'

Megan didn't even look at the woman who had just walked into the toilets. 'Yes,' she fibbed.

'You don't look it. Can I get you a glass of water or something?'

'No, but thanks for offering.' She looked up, this time, and recognised the concerned-looking woman in front of her. Flora Loveday, the school nurse. 'I'll be fine. Just a bit of a headache.' And a whole lot of heartache, otherwise known as Dr Josh O'Hara. Megan forced a smile to her face. 'Are you having a nice time tonight?'

Flora simply glowed. 'Yes. Tom's danced with me all night.'

'Tom the firefighter? He's lovely.' Megan had worked with him a couple of times. He reminded her of Josh—everybody's friend, full of good humour and charm—except she didn't think that Tom was the type to lie, the way Josh had lied to her.

'Yes. I still can't believe how lucky I am. I never expected to find…' Flora paused, looking dismayed. 'Megan? What's wrong?'

Megan scrubbed the tear away. 'I'm fine.' There wasn't a cure for heartache. Unless she could excise Josh from her heart—and she hadn't managed to do that in eight years of trying. 'I think I'll get a taxi home.'

'Let me call it for you, and I'll sit with you while you're waiting,' Flora offered. 'Have you taken anything for your headache yet?' She rummaged in her handbag. 'I've got some paracetamol, if you need it.'

'No, I just need some fresh air and some sleep. You know how busy things get at a hospital.'

'True,' Flora agreed.

Megan splashed water on her face, then called a taxi on her mobile phone.

Flora went out to the reception area with her; on the way, she caught Tom's eye and gestured that she'd be a few minutes. She saw Megan into the taxi, then went back to Tom, who was sitting back at their table, chatting to his friends.

'Everything all right?' he asked as she joined him.

'Megan—you know, the paediatrician from St Piran's?— had a bit of a headache. I waited with her until her taxi arrived.'

'That's my Flora,' Tom said softly, stealing a kiss. 'Looking after everyone.'

'Do you mind?'

'It's one of the things I adore about you,' Tom said, stroking her face. 'My adorable Flora.'

They danced together for the rest of the evening; and Flora found herself disappointed when the band finally stopped playing.

'Come on. I'll drive you home,' Tom said.

Flora was still high on dancing with him all evening. Enough to take a risk when she'd unlocked the front door. She hadn't quite finished knocking his socks off, yet. 'Tom, your parents are with Joey tonight, aren't they?'

'Yes.'

'Are they expecting you home?'

He went very still. 'What are you asking, Flora?'

'I'm asking you to stay the night with me.' She lifted her chin. 'To sleep with me. And wake up with me.'

He moistened his lower lip. 'Are you sure about that?'

'Very sure.'

He smiled. 'Give me two minutes to make a phone call.'

'And I'll let Banjo out while you're doing that.'

By the time she'd called the dog back in and locked the front door, Tom had finished his call.

'OK?' she asked.

He nodded.

She smiled. 'Good. And now I'm taking you to bed.' She took his hand and led him up the stairs to her room. The curtains were already drawn but she didn't put the overhead light on; instead, she switched on a string of fairy lights that she'd draped above the bed earlier.

'Wow. This is like a princess's boudoir,' Tom said.

'Which makes you Prince Charming, yes?'

'Me, I'm just a humble firefighter,' he said with a grin.

'No, you're gorgeous. And you're all mine.'

He laughed. 'If this is what champagne does to you, remind me to keep a bottle in the fridge at all times.'

'It's not the champagne,' she said. 'It's you.' He'd given her the confidence that made her feel as if she could do anything.

Slowly, she undressed him; she untied his bow-tie first, then removed his jacket.

Tom tried to undo the zip at the back of her dress but she wagged a finger at him. 'Uh-uh. I'm in charge.'

Her face was very serious; Tom hid his amusement, not wanting to hurt her. Flora couldn't be bossy if she tried. But he liked the surge of confidence; tonight, she simply sparkled. 'In that case, honey, I'm completely in your hands—do what you want with me.'

'Good.' She plugged her MP3 player into a set of speakers by her bed, and soft jazz filled the room. She stood on tiptoe and kissed him, then finished undoing the buttons of his shirt, sliding the material off his shoulders.

He waited for her to hang it over the back of a chair, knowing that she was the tidy sort.

As if she'd guessed what he was thinking, she gave a grin and tossed it over her shoulder, just to prove that she didn't always run to type. She explored his chest with her fingertips, moving in tiny circles across his skin; he caught his breath as her hands moved lower, to his abdomen.

'Nice six-pack, Mr Nicholson,' she said.

And then his mouth went dry as she undid the button and zip of his formal trousers.

'Gorgeous,' she breathed.

'Flora.' He had to stop himself grabbing her; he knew she wanted to be in charge and he had to be patient—even though right then he really wanted to pick her up and lay her back against the pillows before easing into her.

Slowly, slowly, she eased the material of his trousers over his hips.

He helped her then, kicking his shoes off and stepping out of his trousers, pulling his socks off at the same time.

'Turn round,' she said.

He did so, in a slow pirouette.

'Just gorgeous,' she said. 'Tom, you're perfect.'

'That's pretty much what I think about you,' he said. 'And, pretty as your dress is, I really want to take it off.'

She shook her head. 'You'll have to wait. I have other plans.'

He had no idea what she had in mind, but he was definitely playing by her rules tonight. 'I'm in your hands,' he told her.

She pulled the duvet aside and patted the pillows. 'Lie down.'

He did so, and she stood at the end of the bed, swaying to the music. His mouth went dry as she slowly, slowly peeled off her dress.

'Oh, wow. That lace stuff…it's gorgeous.' And he was desperate to take it off her.

She gave him a shy smile. 'You like it?'

'Very much. You're beautiful, Flora.'

She finished peeling off everything except her knickers, then sashayed over towards him.

'I need to touch you, Flora.' His voice was hoarse with need.

She glanced down at his underpants, which were hiding absolutely nothing. 'Mmm. I can see that.'

His breath hissed. 'Flora.'

She held up a finger. 'Wait.' She went to the drawer of the cabinet by her bed, opened it, and withdrew a condom. 'I think we might need this.'

Flora had bought condoms?

He must have spoken aloud, because she looked hurt. 'I'm not that staid and boring, Tom.'

'No, of course you're not.' He leaned forward and kissed her lightly. 'Just that it's my job to take care of you.'

'This is the twenty-first century. And I'm not fat, frumpy Flora any more.'

'You're gorgeous, curvy, incredibly sensual Flora,' he said. 'And I really, really need to touch you.' He dragged in a breath. 'I really, really need you to touch me. Before I implode.' He took her hand and tugged her towards him.

To his pleasure, she climbed onto the bed and straddled him. She manoeuvred him so she could remove his underpants, and then the only thing between them was the lace of her incredibly pretty knickers. He could feel the heat of her sex against his skin, and it sent him dizzy. 'Flora. I'm begging. Please?'

She ripped open the foil packet and slid the condom over his penis. Her hand was shaking slightly, but she was completely in control—and he was happy to let her take the lead, loving the new confidence she was showing.

She lifted herself slightly, drew the material of her knickers to one side, positioned him at her entrance and then slowly, slowly lowered herself onto him.

She leaned forward and touched her mouth to his before rising and lowering herself back on to him. As her arousal grew, she tipped her head back; Tom shifted so he could kiss her throat. He could feel the pulse beating hard there, just like his own heart was racing with desire and need and...*love*.

He felt her start to ripple round him, and he was lost.

'My adorable Flora. I love you,' he whispered, and kissed her hard as his climax shuddered through him.

She looked completely stunned.

'Are you OK?' he asked, wrapping his arms round her and holding her close.

'Yes.' She frowned. 'Did you just say what I think you said?'

He nodded. 'I'm sorry. I know it's fast. I know it's crazy. But my mum said something last weekend, something I know now is just so true. She said when you meet the right one, you *know*. And I do.'

'You love me,' she said in wonder.

'I love all of you, from those beautiful soft curls down to your pearl-pink toenails and everything in between. All that you are, I love,' he said softly.

Her eyes filled with tears. 'Oh, Tom. I love you, too.'

'Good.' He smiled. 'I was hoping you'd say that.'

Tom dealt with the condom, then switched off the music and the lights. Flora cuddled into him, resting her head on his shoulder; and he drifted off to sleep with his arms wrapped round her, feeling warmer and more at peace than he could ever remember.

CHAPTER THIRTEEN

FLORA woke the next morning in Tom's arms. He was already awake, and smiled down at her. 'Good morning, sleepyhead. How's the hangover?'

'What hangover?'

'The champagne you drank, last night,' he reminded her.

'I didn't drink that much,' she said with a smile. 'It wasn't champagne that made me all giddy. That was you.'

'I know the feeling—that's what you do to me.' He stole a kiss. 'I love you, Flora.'

She'd never get tired of hearing this. Never. 'I love you, too,' she said softly.

'So what are we doing today?'

'Much as I'd like to stay here with you all day, that's not an option.' She paused. 'Aren't your parents going back to France this evening?'

'Yes.'

'Then how about I cook us all Sunday lunch,' she said, 'and we spend the afternoon on the beach making sandcastles with Joey until they have to go?'

Tom held her close. A day with all the people he loved. *His family.* 'That,' he said, 'sounds absolutely perfect.'

'Turnout, vehicles 54 and 55. RTC.' There was a pause. 'Cutting gear needed.'

Road traffic collision.

Given the cold snaps they'd had over the winter, Tom had had to face several car accidents since he'd lost his sister to one. But this was the first time since then that they'd been told up front that they'd need cutting gear.

Please, God, let them be able to free the trapped and get everyone safely to hospital. Don't let another family have to go what his had gone through.

It turned out to be only one vehicle involved, wrapped round a tree. It looked as if the driver had hit black ice and spun off the road.

'The ambulance is on its way but we need to check out the driver now. Tom, you've got the ALS training,' Steve said.

'OK, Guv. I'm on it.' The passenger's side of the car was bent round the tree; Tom tried the driver's door, but it was jammed. He tried the rear passenger door, and to his relief it opened.

There wasn't a huge amount he could do before the ambulance arrived, but he could do the basics. ABCDE—airway, breathing, circulation, disability, exposure.

'I'm Tom, one of the fire crew,' he said, leaning in through the back door. 'The ambulance is on its way and we're going to get you out, mate. What's your name?'

'Ethan.'

The driver could speak, which meant his airway was clear. His breathing seemed a bit shallow, but Tom couldn't get a proper look to see if Ethan was losing any blood. ABC. D: disability. There were no immediate neurological problems, he thought, because Ethan had been able to answer a question. But as for exposure, checking the extent of his injuries—that would have to wait until they'd cut him out.

'Do you have any pain anywhere, Ethan?' Tom asked.

'My neck,' Ethan said.

Could be whiplash; could be a spinal injury. 'As soon as

the ambulance is here, we'll get a collar on you and get you out. Anywhere else?'

'My legs. My foot's stuck.'

The front of the car had crumpled, so Ethan's foot was probably caught between the pedals. They'd need the cutters to get him out—and they'd have to take the roof off the car to move him.

'We'll get you out of here soon. Can you remember what happened?'

'I was late for a meeting—then the car fishtailed and I was heading straight for the tree.'

Which sounded like a classic case of black ice. Given that he was running late, Ethan probably hadn't been giving his full concentration to the road; black ice was tough to spot at the best of times, but when you weren't looking for it you didn't stand a chance. Tom glanced into the car's interior. He couldn't see any passengers, but he needed to check. 'Were you on your own in the car?' he asked.

'Yes,' Ethan said.

'OK. I'm going to talk to my station manager about the best way to get you out. I'll be back in two minutes.' Steve was already assessing the car when Tom went to talk to him. 'Possible spinal injury, and his foot's stuck.'

'We're going to have to open the car for the ambo crew so they can get a board in, then,' Steve said. 'And probably cut the pedals to free him. Right. Let's stabilise the car.'

'I'll tell him what we're doing.' Tom leaned into the back of the car again. 'Ethan, we're going to make the car safe so it won't move, and then the paramedics are going to get you out, OK?'

'Uh-huh.'

The first emergency vehicle to arrive wasn't the ambulance, as Tom had expected, but the rapid response unit car. Josh O'Hara climbed out of the front seat.

'Hey, Tom. Looks nasty. What have we got?'

'Just the driver—his name's Ethan. He's talking, but the front's jammed so I can't tell if he's bleeding or how badly he's injured. His neck hurts and his foot's trapped.'

'If I get a collar on him, can you cut him out?'

'Sure.'

While Josh sorted out the collar, Tom and the rest of the fire crew sorted the rams and spreaders.

'Can you sit with him while we cut him out?' Tom asked.

'Course I will.'

Tom handed him the blue tear-shaped plastic shield and leaned into the back. 'Ethan, we're going to cut you out so the doctor can take a proper look at you. It's going to be noisy in here, but don't worry—Josh is going to stay with you. We have to cut through the windscreen, so Josh is going to hold a shield in front of you to make sure you don't get any glass in your face.'

'Uh-hmm.' Ethan's voice sounded slurred and Tom exchanged a concerned glance with Josh.

'Ten minutes and you'll be out of here,' Tom said.

By the time they'd cut him out, the ambulance crew had the trolley next to the car, ready to take Ethan in, and Josh had got a line into him so the all-essential fluids could go in. Tom put a shield over Ethan's legs to protect him, then used the cutter to snap the pedal trapping his legs. After that, the paramedics took over, getting a spinal board on Ethan, then taking him off to St Piran's.

Josh looked at Tom. 'You OK?'

'Yeah.' Just. And he knew why Josh had asked. 'I admit, it's making me think of my sister. And I just wish…' But wishing couldn't make things right. Couldn't bring her back.

Josh laid a hand on Tom's shoulder. 'I'm sorry, mate. There's nothing anyone can do or say to fix it.'

'No.' Tom looked at Josh. 'You don't look so good yourself. Is this bringing back memories for you, too?'

'No. It's just that life can be so... Have you ever done something you really, really regret later?'

Josh was usually the life and soul of the football match, joking and laughing afterwards. And Tom had the strongest feeling that his friend was doing exactly the same as Tom himself had always done: using laughter as a shield to hide his emotions. It looked to him as if Josh needed to talk to someone. And it might as well be him. 'Look, it's practically lunchtime,' he said. 'You must be due a break, too.'

'Well, yeah.'

'Fancy grabbing a sandwich?'

Josh shook his head. 'A sandwich won't do. Even if it comes with chunky fries.'

'If it's a serious carb fix you need, how about pizza?'

'That,' Josh said, 'would definitely work for me.'

'OK. See you at Luigi's in twenty minutes?'

'You're on.'

Twenty minutes later Josh walked into the pizza parlour to see Josh already there. Josh ordered a pizza loaded with absolutely everything, and wisecracked his way through the whole meal. Tom waited until their coffees had arrived, then said gently, 'OK. You do the same as I do—tell enough jokes and it'll all go away. Except it doesn't.' He paused. 'So what's happened?'

Josh sighed. 'It's messy.'

'I'm not going to spill to anyone. Tell me,' Tom encouraged him.

'Years ago, I fell for someone. It went wrong—and it was my fault.' A muscle flickered in Josh's jaw. 'I never forgot her, but there was no way we were going to be together.'

'And you got married on the rebound?' Tom asked. He'd heard the rumours that Josh's marriage was in trouble, and his wife never appeared at the football matches nowadays. Tom had met Rebecca a couple of times; she was nice enough, but maybe a little too picture-perfect.

Josh sighed. 'No. I loved Rebecca, thought I did, but if I'm honest I know I never felt the same connection with her as I did with my ex. We've been drifting apart for years.' He looked grim. 'I don't think our marriage can be saved and I don't think either of us really wants to try saving it.'

'So you're looking at divorce?'

'I guess so. We want different things out of life. She wants a baby above all else.'

'And I take it you don't?'

Josh grimaced. 'I've never wanted kids—never—and she knows that. We had a deal.' He blew out a breath. 'And now I've done something really stupid. I got drunk at the dinner on Saturday night. And…you know how it is. You're tired, you're not thinking about what you're doing. She was warm, she was there—and, God help me.' He raked a hand through his hair. 'I shouldn't have done it. It wasn't fair to her. I didn't use a condom—and she didn't stop me.'

Tom looked at him in sympathy. 'Have you talked to her about it since?'

'No. She's pretending it never happened, but we both know it did. And we both know why it happened, too.' Josh sighed. 'This is crazy. I don't love her any more, and she doesn't love me. I ought to let her go, find someone who'll give her what she wants.'

'And you're still thinking about the girl you lost?' Tom guessed.

'It would help,' Josh said drily, 'if I didn't have to work with her.'

Tom blew out a breath. 'Tricky one. Does she know you still have feelings for her?'

'I'm not sure. She won't discuss it with me. On Saturday,

she told me to go home to my wife. And, like an idiot, I did. And…' He sighed. 'Rebecca knew I was drunk, that I wasn't thinking straight. And I'll never forgive myself if we've made a baby.'

'She's not on the Pill?'

'She was,' Josh said, but his tone made it clear he didn't think she was any more.

'It doesn't always happen first time,' Tom said. 'You're a doctor. You know the odds.'

'Yeah.' Josh drained his coffee. 'Well, enough of my problems. How are things with Joey?'

'He's really started to open up to me,' Tom said. 'Funny, I used to be like you. I never thought I wanted kids. But now I'm Joey's stand-in dad…and I'm getting used to it. More than that, I'm actually enjoying it.'

'And you have Flora. She's a sweetheart.'

'A definite keeper,' Tom said.

'I hope it works out for you,' Josh said. He glanced at his watch. 'And we'd better get back on shift. See you at the game on Sunday?'

'Absolutely. And we're going to beat you four-nil,' Tom said with a grin.

'In your dreams.' Josh clapped him on the shoulder. 'Thanks, mate.'

'I didn't do a lot.'

'You listened. It helped.'

Though, seeing the shadows in his friend's eyes, Tom wasn't so sure.

'Good day?' Flora asked as Tom walked in.

'Sort of.' He ruffled Joey's hair, made a fuss of Banjo, then came to steal a kiss from Flora. 'I had to cut someone out of a car today.'

Joey went very still.

'He skidded on the ice,' Tom said gently, 'but he was all right. He wasn't very well when he got to hospital, but they made him better. He's got a sore shoulder and a broken ankle, but the doctors told me he's going to be fine.'

'That's good.' Flora put a mug of tea in front of him.

'I've been thinking,' he said. 'I'm going to resign from the fire service.'

'What?' She stared at him. 'Why? You love your job. It's who you are.'

'I know.' He wrinkled his nose. 'But I think it's the only way.'

'The only way to do what, Tom?'

'I know what I want out of life. I want to be a family with you both,' Tom said. 'And my job's dangerous. It's not fair to make you take on that burden.'

'Tom, we love you for who you are—and you've always been a firefighter. It's what you've always wanted to do. You'd be miserable doing anything else.'

'Maybe.' He looked at Flora and Joey. 'But you're worth it.'

'Don't we get a say in this?' Flora asked.

Tom frowned. 'How do you mean?'

'We know what you do is dangerous but it's an important job. Provided you don't take stupid risks—and you know exactly what I mean by that—I can handle it,' she told him. 'Joey?'

Joey frowned. Then he said, 'I love you, Tom.'

Tom stared at him, completely unable to speak. A month ago, Joey had barely been stringing two words together and had hated being touched; he never, but never spoke about anything emotional. And now, unless his hearing had suddenly gone skewy...

He glanced at Flora, and knew that he'd definitely heard Joey say it.

I love you.

'I love you too, sweetheart,' he whispered.

'If your fire engine had gone to rescue my mum and dad, they'd still be here instead of going to heaven,' Joey said.

Tom felt as if his soul had just been flayed. The little boy had that much confidence in him? And yet, even though Tom knew he was incredibly committed to his job, he wasn't sure that he could've saved Susie and Kevin. Nobody could've been pulled out of a collision like that. 'Joey, sweetheart, I don't know if anyone could've saved them,' he said softly.

'But if anyone could, you could,' Joey said. 'And I don't want someone else to lose their mum and dad because you're not on the team any more.'

'Out of the mouths of babes,' Flora said. 'He's got a point. You're good at what you do. No, you're amazing at what you do.'

'But wouldn't you both be happier if I had a less dangerous job—something that didn't risk my life?' he asked.

Flora and Joey looked at each other, clearly considering it, then shook their heads in unison.

'I'd still be worrying about you,' Flora said, 'but I'd be worrying that you were unhappy, not that you were in danger.'

'So you'd be OK if I stayed as a firefighter?' He could really have it all—a family *and* his career? It was really that easy? He'd spent days and days trying to work out what he should do, ever since Flora had made him realise that he had to consider Joey before he took the more dangerous risks. And he'd come to the conclusion that there wasn't a middle way—that he'd have to give up who he was.

And now, it seemed, he didn't.

Joey nodded. 'You're really cool, Uncle Tom.'

'I second that,' Flora said.

Banjo barked, as if to third it, and Flora and Joey laughed.

'If we're a family,' Joey said, 'does that mean we'll all live here with Banjo?'

'Would you like that?' Tom asked.

Joey nodded. 'You'd be like my dad and Flora would be like my mum. That'd be cool. And then you'd have a baby.'

'A baby?' Flora asked, looking surprised.

'Because that's what people do when they get married. Have babies. And I'd be a big brother.' He beamed. 'That'd be cool, too.'

Tom thought of Flora, pregnant with his child, and sheer desire surged through him. 'Sounds good to me. Flora?'

She coughed. 'Is that a proposal, Tom Nicholson?'

He smacked his forehead. 'I'm meant to be down on one knee, and there should be champagne and diamonds and—'

'And none of that's important,' Flora interrupted. 'What's important is exactly what Joey said.'

'So how about it? Would you marry us and be a family with us?'

'Would you?' Joey said. 'And can we live here?'

Flora smiled at them. 'I can't think of anything in the world I'd rather do. Yes.'

Tom picked her up and swung her round, Joey whooped with glee, and Banjo barked madly. And when he set her back down on her feet, he enfolded Joey in a hug along with Flora. 'My family,' he said. 'My perfect dream come true.'

Medical Romance™

HER LITTLE SECRET
by Carol Marinelli

At Eastern Beach Hospital new doctor Nick Roberts' fun-loving attitude is so infectious that nurse Alison Carter is unwillingly hooked. One night with Nick leaves Alison with a new zest for life—and one rather more unexpected gift…

THE DOCTOR'S DAMSEL IN DISTRESS
by Janice Lynn

There's something about nurse Madison's unawakened sex appeal that has Dr Levi Fielding *desperate* to have her in his arms. So when Levi saves Madison's life at a hospital picnic, he knows it's a white knight moment he'll take *full* advantage of…

THE TAMING OF DR ALEX DRAYCOTT
by Joanna Neil

Dr Alex Draycott has plenty on her plate—even before she meets the rebelliously charming Dr Callum Brooksby! Feisty Alex can handle a challenge—but it seems Callum is out to tame her heart…

THE MAN BEHIND THE BADGE
by Sharon Archer

However new-doc-in-town Kayla Morgan tries, she can't resist being impressed by law-enforcing Tom Jamieson! But taking a bullet in the line of duty has made cop Tom rethink his work hard/party harder lifestyle—will he ever let Kayla see the real man behind the badge?

On sale from 6th May 2011
Don't miss out!

Available at WHSmith, Tesco, ASDA, Eason and all good bookshops
www.millsandboon.co.uk

2 FREE BOOKS
AND A SURPRISE GIFT

We would like to take this opportunity to thank you for reading this Mills & Boon® book by offering you the chance to take TWO more specially selected books from the Medical™ series absolutely FREE! We're also making this offer to introduce you to the benefits of the Mills & Boon® Book Club™—

- **FREE home delivery**
- **FREE gifts and competitions**
- **FREE monthly Newsletter**
- **Exclusive Mills & Boon Book Club offers**
- **Books available before they're in the shops**

Accepting these FREE books and gift places you under no obligation to buy, you may cancel at any time, even after receiving your free books. Simply complete your details below and return the entire page to the address below. You don't even need a stamp!

YES Please send me 2 free Medical books and a surprise gift. I understand that unless you hear from me, I will receive 5 superb new stories every month including two 2-in-1 books priced at £5.30 each and a single book priced at £3.30, postage and packing free. I am under no obligation to purchase any books and may cancel my subscription at any time. The free books and gift will be mine to keep in any case.

Ms/Mrs/Miss/Mr _____ Initials _____

Surname _____

Address _____

_____

_____ Postcode _____

E-mail _____

Send this whole page to: Mills & Boon Book Club, Free Book Offer, FREEPOST NAT 10298, Richmond, TW9 1BR